BOOKS BY PAIGE DIXON

Promises to Keep
Lion on the Mountain
Silver Wolf
The Young Grizzly

PROMISES TO KEEP

PROMISES TO KEEP

Paige Dixon

Atheneum
1974 New York

Copyright © 1974 by Paige Dixon
All rights reserved
Library of Congress catalog card number 74-75560
ISBN 0-689-30408-0
Published simultaneously in Canada by
McClelland & Stewart, Ltd.
Manufactured in the United States of America
by H. Wolff, New York
First Edition

For my cousin and godson, Michael Tuck,
and his wife Patty.

PROMISES
TO KEEP

1

I WAS SITTING IN THE BARBER CHAIR WHEN I HEARD THAT
Lon was coming to live with us. Or not exactly with us
but with my grandmother, who lived next door. I didn't
hear it from my family. Oh, no, nothing that normal.
I had to hear it from Jerry Malone, town barber
and champion gossip. I was sitting there in a nervous fit
because he always cuts off too much hair, when all of a
sudden he said, "When does that kid get here, Charles?"

"What kid? Jerry, no more off the sideburns, all
right?"

"Your cousin."

"I haven't got a cousin." The Millers are a dying
breed, at least our branch. I'm the last of the line. Except for . . . I turned my head so fast, Jerry almost
nicked my cheek with the shears. "Cousin?"

"You don't know?" He gave me that happy "tsk-tsk"
that means I've made his day because he gets to spill some
news. "Your Uncle Bill's kid. The foreign kid."

I was shocked right down to my feet but I tried not to let it show. I guess I was acting like my grandmother; her attitude always was: "Don't let the peasants see your real feelings. You're a Miller." She didn't actually say "peasants," but that was her attitude.

I played it cool with Jerry. "Oh, yeah. I forgot about him. He'll be here pretty soon, I guess. I didn't pay attention to the details."

It was such a startling piece of news, I even forgot to stare at my ugly face in the mirror as I usually did when I was getting a haircut. In the year or so before, I had developed severe acne, and looking at myself made me feel practically suicidal.

Bill Miller's kid. That foreign kid. Nobody ever said "Bill's son" or "Your cousin, Lon." Not that they hadn't talked about him plenty when they discovered he existed. When Uncle Bill came home that one time and announced that he had married a Vietnamese girl almost seven years before, and they had a six-year-old son, Grandmother nearly had a stroke, literally, and the town buzzed for months. "Poor Mrs. Miller, at her age." "How have the mighty fallen." Et cetera. Of course they always added that naturally the girl must be a prostitute, and maybe they weren't even legally married. That was in 1966 before people knew as much about Vietnam as they think they do now, but even that long ago everybody in Miller's Lake, New Hampshire, knew what Oriental women were like.

When Grandmother held up her head and refused to discuss Bill's marriage, that made the locals resent the

Millers more than ever. "Who does she think she is, Queen of New Hampshire?"

At the time I was only nine years old, but you can put a lot of twos and twos together at that age. People in the family stopped talking when I came into the room, but I learned to sidle in slowly and silently, picking it all up in chapters like a TV soap opera. And at school, kids insulted me about my slope cousin, the gook, and all that. It is a very liberal-minded community, with charity in their hearts and malice toward none. Ha!

After a while the talk died down, but Uncle Bill was killed and it flared up like a fire that hadn't really died out. What would happen? Would Mrs. Miller give the kid and the prostitute (it wasn't even said she *might* be a prostitute now) house room? There was a lot of grumbling about what people would do if this happened. Actually they wouldn't have done anything out in the open. It was too much of a town custom to stand in awe of Grandmother. After all, the Millers had founded the town (for whatever that might be worth), and for years everybody's father, grandfather, uncle, or son had worked for the Millers unless they worked for the railroad. That was all there was, the Millers' cotton mill and the railroad. Both of them gone now, but the attitudes lingered on.

I don't know what Grandmother would have done if Lon's mother had said they were coming. She'd have had a real conflict between her Christian conscience, which was about as flexible as the Berlin wall, and her sense of outrage. But they didn't come. They moved to Hawaii, and there was a large sigh of relief at the Miller hearths.

But now what? I paid Jerry and rode my bike home. My father was messing around in his so-called workshop as usual. Theoretically he was in the real estate business, but since the Boston and Maine quit running trains through our town, nobody ever comes here except the summer people at the lake, who live a life of their own. Like a lot of northern New England small towns, we live in real isolation. Even people looking for a cheap tax rate don't linger in our town, because except for the lake, where there is no property available anymore, Miller's Lake is a very ugly little town, a mill town without a mill. And characters to match.

So we lived off Grandfather's trust fund. My father, who really isn't a bad guy, although he's so ineffectual he makes you want to cry, had all these stupid hobbies. Like woodworking. Cutting up what would have been a perfectly good tree just to make a phony cobbler's bench or a table that never stood quite steady. And most of what it amounted to was heaps of sawdust that I usually had to sweep up.

I got right to the point. "Why didn't you tell me Lon was coming?"

He looked up, with those pale blue eyes (like mine) full of phony surprise. "Oh, didn't you know?"

"How would I know? Short of telepathy." I admit I am not always nice to my father, but he does bug me.

"I thought you'd have heard . . ."

"I did. At the barbershop."

"Oh." He looked mildly distressed. "Yes, he is coming to stay with your grandmother."

"His mother, too?"

My father squinted at the piece of wood on the lathe. What it was for, God only knew. Then he gave me the full-front, straight-from-the-shoulder look. "His mother died, you know."

For some reason this infuriated me. "Why do you say 'you know'?" My voice was louder than I meant it to be, and he flinched. "How would I know? Who ever tells me anything around here?" I was more upset about not being told things than I was about Lon's mother being dead. I didn't even know the woman.

"I'm sorry, son. We just learned it ourselves. Your grandmother didn't feel like talking about it at first. She had to consider her course of action, and you know she likes to do that by herself."

What he meant was, advice to Grandmother is like the proverbial red flag to the bull. Only that's a silly expression because bulls are actually color-blind.

"So we've only just learned it ourselves."

"How did Jerry know it?"

He shrugged. "Probably Hancock talked."

Hancock and his wife worked for Grandmother. Hancock was chauffeur, gardener, handyman; and Mrs. H. was, as my father liked to say, "chief cook and bottle-washer," plus maid and companion and what have you.

My father's cowlick was standing up straight and he looked hot, although it wasn't all that hot; it was only April. "Of course the family must take in Bill's boy. No matter what. It's the only possible procedure."

I could see he was upset. My father suffers from about ninety-four kinds of inadequacy, not the least

7

of which is the feeling that his older brother did everything right and Dad does everything slightly wrong.
Uncle Bill was captain of the football team at Bowdoin,
and a few years later Dad was some kind of manager,
which I gather was roughly equivalent to water boy.
Uncle Bill was tall and good-looking; my father is short
and skinny, although he's not as bad-looking as he thinks
he is. Uncle Bill was in ROTC in college, in the Army
afterward, and eventually went off to the war in Vietnam, when being an "adviser" in the Far East was
glamorous. My father couldn't even get the Army Re-
serve to take him. He's nearsighted and he has asthma.
Uncle Bill was always Grandmother's pride and joy; she
tolerates my father. In her eyes the only bad thing Bill
ever did was to marry "that woman," and she put that
down, finally, to battle fatigue (although in 1958 Uncle
Bill hadn't been in battle) and the scheming wiles of the
girl. "It's a well-known fact," she said, on the one occasion when she mentioned the situation in my presence,
"that Oriental women are unscrupulous." That was
several years ago that she said that.

My father brushed some shavings off his pant leg. "Lon
is only a couple of years younger than you. You'll en-
joy him."

"Sure," I said. "I can hardly wait."

I left him and went into the house. If there was anything I didn't need that spring it was a strange cousin
who'd been ostracized, sight unseen, since the day he was
heard of. This was my first year in the local school in
five years. When I was a kid, I had rheumatic fever and

I lost a year of school. After that I was sent to the Country Day School in another township. That in itself was a point against me. It was said I thought I was too good for the local school. Actually it was Grandmother who decided those things. She thought I needed polish and some basis in the classics. I don't know about the polish, but I got the classics. If anybody wanted to sit up at the drugstore counter with me and swap jests in Latin, I could do myself proud.

Country Day was really all right, but it was small and you got sick of the same old teachers and the same old kids. Besides, there was Patty. So I pressured Grandmother to let me switch to Miller's Lake High that year as a junior, and she finally gave in. Except for the Hancocks, I was the only one who could ever do anything with her, and that wasn't much. I think it's because I have a head shaped like Uncle Bill's and I was no threat to her.

That first year back at Miller's Lake had been really rough. I had an awful lot to live down. In addition to being a Miller and having gone to a private school, I had also grown a foot in a year and I had developed this terrible acne. My mother kept telling me lots of kids had it, but what was that to me? I tried a new medicinal soap a week, and I was even taken to a skin doctor in Boston. Nothing.

So I had to work like a maniac to offset all these disadvantages. I'd made the honor list (not that that does much for you with your peers in Miller's Lake) and I'd been elected president of the debating club. I really shook up that club. I got them to debate topics like: "Resolved: that marriage is archaic." It stirred up some PTA static, but the faculty was so impressed with the fact that kids had gotten interested in debates, they chose to overlook the reasons. I got fencing added to the P.E. program. I'd been a good fencer, but I lost my coordination when I grew so fast. I could still show people how, though.

Everybody thought I'd be a sensational addition to the basketball team because I could practically look down into the baskets, so I tried out and failed horribly. I kept tripping over my own feet and falling down. A basketball player has to be as controlled as a polo pony.

Joey Parrish and his gang made so many snide remarks about my physical prowess that finally in desperation I went out for baseball and made the team. I still was clumsy, but you can get away with that more in baseball, especially if it's a lousy team. I could run fast and, surprisingly, I could pitch pretty well. I got treated with a little more respect after I made the team. Not much but a little.

I even made a couple of friends. And now, after all my hard work, I was going to be saddled with this kid that everybody was programmed to hate. It would probably ruin my life.

2

LON'S PLANE WAS DUE AT LOGAN AIRPORT ON A SATURDAY
at two forty-five in the afternoon. My parents and I
were going to meet him. They were nervous. I came into
the kitchen about 10 A.M. to get some breakfast, and there
was my mother sitting at the table quartering and peeling
an apple. Even under the best of circumstances, my
mother makes a real production out of getting ready to
eat an apple. First she halves it, very carefully, as if the
future of the human race depended on her getting it absolutely symmetrical. Then she divides the halves. Then
she cuts out the core; a slow, careful process, including
tidying up the seeds into a little heap. Then she peels the
sections. By the time she's done all this, you can't believe
she's got strength enough left to eat the thing.

She put down the paring knife and said, "Oh, good
morning, dear. I'll get you some breakfast."

I waved her off. We go through this every day. She

wants to cook me bacon and eggs and all that, and all I want is a huge bowl of cereal and lots of milk. We just don't see eye-to-eye on breakfast at all.

I really like my mother, but she can be exasperating. For one thing, she used to have an idea that my father married beneath him. That's because the Millers have always had the whole town bamboozled into thinking they're straight from Olympus. My mother's father was chief dispatcher when the town was a big railroad terminal, and that's no cinch of a job. He really had to be sharp. In my opinion, which nobody ever asks, that took more brains and nerve than managing an inherited factory, and that was already on the skids anyway. If Grandfather Blaine had gotten absentminded for one second, or if he had had a couple of bourbons for lunch, the way Grandfather Miller used to do, there could have been a train wreck. The big freights used to go through here, lots of them. And passenger trains fanned out from here all over northern New England. Sometimes I go down to the station, which is deserted now, and sit on the platform and look at that big mess of tracks and think how exciting it used to be. It's too bad we gave up on trains. Now you can't even get in here without a car.

But about my mother. Because she felt she wasn't quite up to the Millers, she was always kind of apologetic about everything, and she let Grandmother Miller really boss her around. Her mother was the same; a very nice woman, and a great cook, but kind of rabbity.

"It will be exciting to see your cousin, won't it?" my mother said.

I spilled some milk. I nearly always spilled the milk. It was almost a compulsion. After I mopped it up, I answered her. "I don't know. To tell you the truth, I'd just as soon he'd stayed in Hawaii."

My mother looked distressed. She is kindhearted to the point of ridiculousness. She suffers with everybody, even people she's never even seen. Sometimes my father and I try to keep the newspaper away from her, so she won't get all choked up over some miner who died in a cave-in in West Virginia or some kid who ran away from home.

"He must be feeling very sad," my mother said, speaking of Lon. "He's an orphan now. He must miss his mother terribly."

I made no comment. If my mother was thinking of Lon as an orphan, nothing would be too good for him.

"I hope your grandmother will be fond of him."

"You know she won't. She'll take it out on him that Uncle Bill married a native."

"Don't say 'native,'" she said. "That's a stupid word. We're all natives of wherever we live."

I'd never thought of that before. Sometimes my mother surprises me.

"Life won't be easy for that boy," she said. "You help him all you can, Charles."

My father came in the back door just as I was finishing breakfast. "We'd better get going. Weekend traffic, you know."

"It'll be going north," I said. He always wants to get an early start, and then we sit and wait on the other end.

But he hovered around looking nervous, so my mother and I got ourselves together.

He jingled the car keys. "All set-o?" Ever since I can remember, he's said that, "all set-o." What kind of a thing is that for a grown man to say?

My mother sat in the back seat because I used to get carsick when I was a kid, and the memories were still vivid enough that nobody wanted to take any chance on putting me in back.

My father whistled awhile, and then he talked to me about the basketball team. He hates team sports but he thinks I love them. I hate them even more than he does, because I have to play them.

I was thinking about the last time I went to Logan. Six months ago, to see Patty Henderson and her parents off to Germany. Patty was one of the major reasons why I negotiated the switch to Miller's Lake High. She was the only girl who'd go out with me after I got into my ugly stage. She loved me for my mind. Actually she wasn't any beauty queen either, but one thing my experience with Patty taught me was, a girl is like a Christmas present: if the present has pretty wrapping, that's nice but it's not necessarily very permanent; it's what's inside the package that counts. How do you like that? Move over for the Kahlil Gibran of Miller's Lake, New Hampshire. Pearls of wisdom, man.

Anyway, all I got out of changing schools for Patty was a nice letter once a month (getting a little further apart each month) and some pretty good German stamps. I missed her. She was the only person for a long time that I'd talked to about wanting to be a writer. That just wasn't the kind of thing I wanted bruited about in Miller's Lake. In Miller's Lake, a writer, if he's male, is bound to be a nut or a queer or both. Artists and musicians likewise. Unless, of course, they make a lot of money. Anyway, my grandmother would have flipped if she'd known I wanted to be a writer. She had plans for me. She'd tried to get Uncle Bill into West Point or Annapolis and failed. Now I was the candidate. Our family is full of military tradition. People will tell you the military bit is out, but they don't know Miller's Lake. The Legion and the VFW are the most important groups in town, and Memorial Day is more popular than Christmas.

I was beginning to get a headache from my father's driving. He likes to cruise along about fifty-five, and then with no warning he shoots up to seventy. You get yourself together for seventy, and he drops back to fifty. No reason.

By the time we got to the big cloverleaf near the Air Force base, and my father was fumbling for the toll change, which he never has, I was beginning to feel what my mother calls quasi-queasy. There's no way to stop on that turnpike without causing havoc, especially if my father did it, so I searched in my jacket pocket for a peppermint lifesaver and a couple of aspirins. I heard my mother say, "Oh dear," and I knew she knew I was feeling sick.

I concentrated on other things. I have almost, but not quite, learned to will myself out of feeling sick. The trouble is, if you relax your concentration for even a second, you're in trouble.

I thought we'd never get to Boston, but finally we did, and I shut my eyes so I wouldn't have to watch the things my father does in traffic. How we've all lived so long, I'll never understand.

"There," he said finally, swooping into a parking slot at the terminal. "All hunky-dory and in plenty of time."

Of course we actually had forty-five minutes to wait, even if the plane was on time. I told them I'd meet them at the gate, and I took off before anybody could object. I walked around in the cool air for a while, till my stomach and my head began to settle down, and then I went up to the observation deck to watch the planes. Logan is a wild airport. On the approach, you're practically in the water. And downtown Boston is within spitting distance. I like it, though.

I caught up with my parents at the gate, just as the plane was taxiing up. They both looked scared, and I felt very funny myself. Suddenly I was hoping and praying the kid would look like Uncle Bill. It would be so much easier for everybody to accept him. And for one moment I felt awfully sorry for him. He must be scared to death. He'd never even been stateside before. But then I braced myself for the worst as people began coming out of the corridor that connected with the plane. He'd probably be wearing a gaudy Hawaiian shirt and sandals and be grinning from ear to ear like a Chinese laundryman in one of those old movies. Only of course he wasn't Chinese.

Almost everybody was out of the plane, and there'd been no sign of anybody who might be Lon. My mother and father looked at each other anxiously. "Somebody should have met him on the West Coast," my mother said. "He's only a child."

My father said, "Mildred, the boy is fourteen. And who could go clear to the West Coast?"

"But he's just lost his mother, and he doesn't know this country . . ."

"There he is," I said.

He was standing in the doorway, looking at us. He was fairly tall for his age, and slender, not really thin, just slender. He was wearing a lightweight dark suit, a good suit, with a wide black band on the arm. I had never seen anyone wear a mourning band except our chaplain at Country Day, when his mother died, and he was English. Lon had on a button-down white shirt and a conservative tie. His hair was shorter than mine, very black and silky and flat to his head. He had a ukelele under his arm and a flight bag in his hand. A ukelele! My father had one of those when he was in college.

My mother started toward Lon. He gave her a little smile, but he didn't rush into her arms or anything. He looked very Oriental. He had pale skin and big black eyes with that strange little tuck in the corner that Orientals have. He was poised, so poised it kind of annoyed me. I'd been all ready to help out this poor little foreign orphan, but he didn't seem to need my help at all.

"I'm Lon," he said to my mother. Which seemed obvious.

17

My mother, who is a very sentimental woman, threw her arms around him. I saw him stiffen and it made me mad. I don't like to be hugged either, but who was he to reject my mother? Nobody else seemed to notice it. Dad was pumping his hand as if it was the balky pump handle at the cottage. "So glad to see you, my boy," he kept saying, and my mother was all tearful. Lon looked past them at me, a very calm, searching look. It made me very uneasy. I supposed he was thinking, "So that's my cousin. That big, overgrown bunch of blemishes."

I didn't offer to shake hands. I didn't want him stiffening up on me. I just said, "Hi."

"Hi," he said. "You're Charles."

We stood looking at each other. If it wasn't such a faggotty thing to have thought, I'd have said to myself he was beautiful, in a very exotic kind of way.

Sometimes I get these flashes of fantasy. Instead of seeing what's really in front of me, I see another scene altogether, just for an instant. I know it isn't real; I'm sane enough for that; but for the moment it is very vivid.

Looking at Lon, I suddenly saw him as a statue in a big museum. Marble. Very beautiful and graceful. People standing off at a distance looking at him, and somebody saying in an incredulous voice, "He can't be Charles Miller's cousin."

The fantasy dissolved, and there he stood with his ukelele in his hand and his button-down shirt. Charles Miller's cousin, well-proportioned and with not one single pimple.

While we stood around waiting for his luggage, I noticed we were all nervous except Lon. Or if he was, it didn't show. My father chattered and laughed a lot and said things like, "Charles can't wait to challenge you to a tennis game." I had never even thought of challenging him to a tennis game.

Lon smiled and said, "I like tennis."

My mother cooed about how tired he must be and was he suffering from jet lag. He said he wasn't.

I didn't say much of anything; I just tried to look casual and semifriendly. No point in overdoing the friendship bit, giving him ideas about us being Damon and Pythias. For one thing, he was only fourteen. I wondered what year they'd put him in school.

Finally the luggage came, and I noticed it included a tennis racket. When we got out to the car, he and my mother got in the back. She had to tell him, of course, that I got carsick if I sat in the back.

I gave him what I hoped was a bored smile. "I haven't been carsick for ten years," I said. "But the tradition persists."

He laughed, and I wasn't sure if it was at me or with me. Probably at. He had a surprisingly low voice for a kid his age; quite a nice voice, actually. I wondered if he sang, with that ukelele and all. Uncle Bill used to be a college glee club baritone. But it was hard to think of Lon as belonging to Uncle Bill.

Dad wanted to take us to Durgin-Park for steaks. "Let's show Lon the real Boston," he said. My mother reminded him it was midafternoon, and Lon said he wasn't hungry because they had fed him practically non-stop from Honolulu.

"Mrs. Hancock has been cooking for days, for your arrival," my mother said.

Lon asked politely who Mrs. Hancock was, and both my parents filled him in. Lovely people; devoted to Grandmother; had adored Uncle Bill; been with the family forever; real Yankee types. Mrs. Hancock was Grandmother's only close friend, at least in New Hampshire, but they didn't say that.

"Just don't tell them anything you don't want circulated all over town before nightfall," I said.

"Oh, Charles," my mother said. "They do love to talk, though, Lon."

"No harm meant," my father said. "They wouldn't harm a flea."

"But if you aren't a flea, watch out," I said. I didn't mean it. I liked the Hancocks. I just wanted to sound cynical, and I had discovered that Lon laughed when I said those things. I do like to make people laugh, as long as it's not aimed at me.

It seemed to take a long time to get back to Miller's Lake, but at least I didn't get carsick. When we pulled into the driveway of Grandmother's house, I looked back at Lon. He was even paler than he had been before, and his mouth was tense. So he wasn't really all that cool.

Grandmother's house is kind of impressive. It's an eighteenth-century job, built in 1736, to be exact, but added onto at several later dates. The main house is a big white frame with a central chimney. The front door has a carved lintel over the top and bull's-eye glass on each side. The windows have dark green shutters. Then there are two wings, one on each side, and a built-on section in the back where the present kitchen and pantry are. The original kitchen, which has a huge brick fireplace, is used for a kind of library now, with floor-to-ceiling books. It's my favorite room.

The house is on a hill and behind it the land slopes down to a meadow with a brook in it. There are trees all around the meadow except on the far side, where our house is.

I saw Lon taking it all in as Dad pulled up the circular drive in front of the door. I suppose Lon was looking for Grandmother, but I could have told him she wouldn't show up yet. She liked to have people come to her.

Mrs. Hancock came bubbling out of the house, though, talking a-mile-a-minute and flapping her white apron like a big duck. And Mr. H. wasn't far behind, the last of his wispy hair brushed flat against his head and his Adam's apple bobbing up and down.

"Here's Lon," my mother said. Why do people make these ridiculous remarks? "Lon, this is Mr. and Mrs. Hancock."

I couldn't help grinning, wondering if Lon had thought Mrs. Hancock was Grandmother.

Mrs. H. filled up with tears. She is very emotional. "Lon." She wrung his hand. "We're so glad you're here." She looked at Mr. Hancock tearfully. "Bill's boy." As if Mr. Hancock didn't know that. But what she meant was: isn't this a big emotional moment.

Mr. Hancock swallowed, bobbing his Adam's apple up and down very fast. He stuck out his hand. "Welcome home."

I could see that Lon was touched. His eyes got very

black, almost as if he was going to cry too. But he pulled himself together. This kid seemed to be very big on self-control. The inscrutable type. I wondered if he had a temper like mine, or even better, like his father's. Gossip said that Uncle Bill's temper had been a subject for awe throughout the county.

"Thank you," Lon said. "I'm happy to be here."

Well, he'd made it with the Hancocks, and they were good people to have on your side, but they didn't really cut all that much ice. It was Grandmother he'd have to live with and deal with, and I knew how Grandmother felt about him and his mother.

Mr. H. and Dad did the honors with the luggage, Lon wasn't allowed to carry a thing except his ukelele. I must say, I've never gotten that kind of treatment. The prodigal grandson.

Mrs. H. opened the door wider, and we all trooped into the house. Only once you were inside Grandmother's house, you stopped doing anything so boisterous as trooping. You trod softly and watched your feet and minded the bibelots. Not that Grandmother ever yelled at you to be careful. She just lifted her head and shot you a high-voltage look from those blue eyes. That was enough to subdue a raging mob.

Mrs. Hancock ushered us into the big living room, and we all kind of stood around, Lon still holding his uke and trying to look at everything without seeming to. It was a big room, rather formal, with lots of Duncan Phyfe and Hepplewhite. Mother always said I'd inherit, and I happen to like antiques, but now I realized I'd probably be sharing with Lon. Oh, well, there was a lot of stuff. The things I wanted most were two Henry Stubbs prints of jockeys, done in the middle of the nineteenth century, and the grandfather's clock that some ancestor brought from China. It had a lot of brass and it gonged like mad.

Mother sat down on the edge of the yellow wing chair, ready to leap to her feet at the signal. Dad was pointing out to Lon the portrait of our grandfather. Mr. Hancock had disappeared with the bags, and Mrs. H. had gone to tell Grandmother we had arrived. Not that Grandmother could possibly not have known it, unless she was stone-deaf, which she was far from.

Lon said something to Dad, and I realized he had a slight accent. I hadn't noticed it before. It sounded French, but why French? Don't the Vietnamese speak Vietnamese? Lon kept glancing toward the door, and I knew he was getting nervous waiting for Grandmother. She did that on purpose; it gave her an advantage. At least I always thought she did it on purpose. I had never seen her enter a room until everybody else was already there and waiting.

Lon had put down his uke and was standing by the fireplace looking up at the huge crystal chandelier when Mrs. Hancock stuck her head in the door and nodded violently to let us know Grandmother was coming. She scuttled off again, and in about one minute and twenty seconds Grandmother appeared in the doorway. Mother leaped to her feet, and we all stood stock-still like a frozen TV frame. I really liked Grandmother and I was not as scared of her as the others were, but the way they tensed up when she appeared was catching.

She and Lon looked at each other. Grandmother wasn't

so very tall, but she looked tall. I guess "stately" is the word. She had white hair and a young-looking face and fantastic blue eyes. She was impressive.

Lon looked wary, as if he was ready to back up if she came too close. I suppose he thought she might swoop down on him the way Mother and Mrs. H. had done. Not Grandmother. She said, "How do you do, Lon." She shook hands.

"How do you do, Grandmother," he said. He was kind of impressive too. Lots of dignity.

I saw her eyes flick at the word "Grandmother" from him. But what did she expect? "Mrs. Miller"?

She came into the room. "Do sit down, all of you. You must be tired." She sat in the yellow wing chair. My mother perched on the edge of a straight chair. Dad stood with his back to the fireplace, trying to look like a relaxed and self-confident man and failing completely. Lon sat down on the needlepoint bench, and I stood with one foot on the hearth, also trying to look like a relaxed and self-confident man, also not terribly successfully.

"You've had a long trip," Grandmother said.

"Yes, I have," Lon said. He folded his hands together. Very white hands. It was an odd kind of whiteness, his skin, kind of like ivory.

"Mrs. Hancock is making us some tea," Grandmother said. "And afterward I'm sure you will want to go to your room and get settled." To my father she said, "I've put him in the east wing. He'll have privacy there."

The east wing had always held the guest rooms. It was very nice, with a view of the meadow and the mountains. There were two bedrooms and a bath. It would be private, all right. I had taken it for granted she'd put him in Uncle Bill's rooms, which were near hers, but now I realized of course she wouldn't. That would be the last thing she'd do.

Dad talked about the traffic in Boston, and Mother mentioned the new minister at the Congregational Church that the Millers supported. Then the conversation lagged. I wished Mrs. Hancock would hurry up with the tea. Not that I like tea.

My father picked up Lon's ukelele. "Remember when I courted you with one of these things, Mildred?" he said.

My mother smiled and gave my father a look that said "put it down," but he didn't get the message. When he got really nervous with Grandmother, he always tried too hard. He plucked the four strings, tuned them and sang, "My dog has fleas," which he alleges is what you sang when you tuned the strings of your ukelele in his day. I really wouldn't know. I could see that Grandmother was not amused. She was never mean to him or anything, but you got the feeling—and he got it too— that she was putting up with him at great cost to her patience.

"Do they still say 'My dog has fleas'?" Dad said to Lon.

"I don't know. I have never heard that." The accent was strong then, and I saw that Grandmother noticed it.

Then we heard the faint squeak of the tea wagon, and Grandmother said, "Here is Mrs. Hancock."

It was better with the tea. I mean there were things to say and do, like "Can I get you some cream?" and "Charles, see that Lon has a napkin," that sort of thing.

When it was over, Grandmother rose and everybody else rose. "Charlie," she said to my father, "will you show Lon where his room is?" To Lon she said, "Dinner is at seven. If you need anything, there is a bell in your room that connects with the Hancocks' room. They will be glad to help you."

Lon bowed. "Thank you."

My mother said, "Come see us soon, Lon. We're just across the meadow."

He thanked her. My mother thanked Grandmother for the tea. Grandmother thanked my parents for getting Lon. I thanked Grandmother for the tea. She thanked me for getting Lon.

"Will you wait just a minute, Charles, please," she said.

Lon followed my parents into the hall.

"Lon," my grandmother said.

He came back at once, looking expectant. Hoping for what? A kind word?

"You forgot your . . . musical instrument." She said it quietly but you could hear the irritation. She hated clutter.

Lon heard it, too. I saw the dark flash in his eyes, and right away I had another fantasy. Two in one day was very unusual. I saw the flash from Lon's eyes flick around the room like lightning, as if the room wasn't big enough to hold it. I saw the hundreds of pieces of crystal in the chandelier catch fire and throw out rays that sparkled and burned. The room shook with all that voltage.

The image disappeared, and there was Lon politely saying, "Sorry," picking up the uke and leaving the room.

Grandmother watched him go. She sighed and sat down. She generally unwound a little with me. It's not that she was all that fond of me, I suppose, but on the whole I happened not to bug her. And there's that very vague resemblance to Uncle Bill.

"Will you take him to school on Monday, Charles? See that he meets Mr. Ward, and so on."

"Isn't it late for him to start school this year?" I'd taken it for granted I wouldn't have to cope with him at school until fall, and I'd kept hoping she'd send him to Country Day.

"No. He can't just hang around. He must start getting a proper education." To Grandmother, of course, schooling in Hawaii, or anywhere outside New England, would not be a proper education.

"Yes, of course. I'll look after him." Though in my opinion, he didn't need the likes of me.

She nodded, as if she'd stopped listening to me, and stared at the ashes in the fireplace. Then she said, as if to herself, "It's very hard." She looked tired and sad.

When she got up, I walked with her into the hall. "Thank you, Charles. You're a comfort." She took hold of my hand for a second. Hers was cold, and it shook a little.

"Do you feel all right?"

27

"Yes, yes. I'm fine." She gave me a quick little smile and walked away, her back very straight. I suppose she was thinking of Uncle Bill, having Lon show up and all. I hadn't stopped to think how hard on her it probably was. Well, I was on her side.

I ran across the meadow, jumped the brook, slipped and fell flat in the long, wet grass in my new chinos. I picked myself up and went home, thinking, as I often thought, that disaster was just around the corner lying in wait for me. A vague, shadowy, anonymous disaster.

I shut myself in the bathroom and locked the door, and for the next hour I went through my ritual of steaming my face with just-short-of-unendurably hot cloths, applying that week's miracle cure for acne, and so on. It was all so hideously futile. I thought of Lon, washing his unblemished face and going to sleep at night like a normal human being. But maybe not. There are more blemishes in heaven and earth, Horatio . . .

3

YOU COULD HEAR THE FAINT CREAK OF TURNING HEADS AS the Millers marched into church the next morning. We always arrived en masse and always precisely on time. If anything had happened, like getting stuck in the snow some winter morning, to make us late, old Mr. Peters would have held up the service, so that when we walked in, it would still look as if we were on time. I wasn't sure the new minister would be all that cooperative.

Grandmother went first, as she always did, with my mother behind her and my father sort of walking on the backs of my mother's heels, then me. And today, bringing up the rear was Lon. He was wearing the same suit with a different shirt and tie. When we sat down in the Miller pew, I stubbed my toe. I always do. Lon looked around as if he found the church interesting. He didn't seem to know that everybody was sneaking looks at him.

It *was* a nice church. It was old, one of those little white steepled jobs that you see all over New England,

and it had the original pews. There'd been some talk about replacing them, but Grandmother spoke to the Reverend Mr. Peters and the pews were not replaced. Grandmother was the biggest single contributor to the church, in money, although she never did the things my mother does, like serving on committees and breaking her back over the church suppers and all that. They also serve who only bake the beans.

It was clear that Lon was not a Congregationalist. He did everything about half a beat after I did. I imagine Grandmother noticed, although she never seemed to glance our way. Grandmother had a way of feeling things. If it wasn't so un–New Englandish, I'd say she was psychic, but she'd certainly have rejected that idea. I guess she'd think that was Satanism or something. She was kind of an eighteenth-century woman in a lot of ways. She believed in reason and order. I guess that's a good, manageable way to look at life, unless you reach a place where you can't help facing up to chaos. Then it would be a lot more unnerving than if you'd figured all along that life was pretty chaotic.

I was thinking all this stuff as I sat there between Lon and my father, because I make it a practice never to listen to a sermon. I think, instead. Sermons, in my experience, are usually so unreasonable or so downright ridiculous that if you listen to them, they get you so mad that you lose all the nice feeling of being in church. I feel that I have a pretty good relationship with God, and I don't want some stupid minister lousing it up.

But I could tell Lon was listening. I wondered what he thought of whatever Mr. Barnes was saying. I liked Mr.

Barnes even less than I had liked Mr. Peters. Peters was old and doddery, but Barnes was one of these young, with-it ministers, always giving you this sincere smile and urging you to come out for the church volleyball team. In my opinion, if people don't come to church because they're interested in God, there's no use getting them there to play volleyball. That's my opinion. I admit I'm opinionated.

Gerald Dodge was sitting across the aisle, one pew down. I admired Gerald Dodge very much. He knew who he was. He was captain of the football team, president of the student council, and very big in the drama club. He was a senior, already accepted for Yale. He plans to be a lawyer, and he'll probably end up president of the United States or something. I saw him turn his head once during the offertory hymn and give Lon a quick once-over; then he winked at me. I wasn't sure what the wink meant; I suspected it was sympathy, and from anybody else I'd have resented it, but I was pleased that Gerald Dodge paid me that much attention.

After church my father made a big deal of putting his arm around Lon and introducing him to people, especially to people who had kids about Lon's age. He talked so long and so much, in fact, that Grandmother went off without Lon, and we took him home. I wished my father would just shut up and let the whole thing run its course as inconspicuously as possible. I imagine Lon might have agreed with me, but you couldn't tell. He bowed and nodded and shook hands and said, "Thank you. How do you do." Et cetera.

When we left him off, Mr. Hancock came out to say

that Grandmother would like me to show Lon around town after dinner. Now that really burned me up. The baseball team had scheduled practice, and I was supposed to be there. Our team was getting ready to play Wolfeboro. I started to explain this, but my father said, "Of course. Tell my mother Charles will be glad to."

I raged all the way home and more than halfway through dinner. My father looked unhappy, but he wouldn't back down. His theory was that Grandmother wanted it, and that I owed it to my cousin, and he tossed in a reference or two to Uncle Bill's memory.

I was still in a very crabby frame of mind when I picked up Lon. Dad let me take the car as an inducement. Big deal. Lon got in, and I drove him around town, pointing out the local monuments, such as the high school, the junior high school, the elementary school, the public library, the IGA grocery store, the fish market, the ball field, the two bars, the house outside of town—if you could call it a house—where Myrtle Lightbody and her father lived.

"Lightbody. What an odd name. Who are they?"

"Oh, local characters." Actually Myrtle is the town prostitute, and her old man runs a do-it-yourself still. Their house is an old tarpaper shack on the river, outside the town limits.

Lon seemed surprised by the town. I guess he expected a pint-sized New York or something. I tried to explain how isolated and ingrown the town has always been. "And Miller's Lake has delusions of past grandeur—the mill and the railroad and all."

"Do you think," he said, with a small grin, "that the first Miller started the mill because of his name?"

"No. The Millers don't have that kind of imagination."

There was a sputter and a mini-roar as three trail bikes caught up with us. I groaned. It was Joey Parrish and two of his gang. These guys had a club called the Red Flames. They had pitchforks painted on the backs of their jackets, and a clubhouse in an abandoned gas station on the old highway. Joey had tried to get me to join, when he first started the Flames, and he never forgave me for turning him down. I happen not to be a group man, and that kind of thing seemed so childish. Unfortunately I said so. I heard of some pretty weird things going on out at the clubhouse, but I don't know how true any of it was. My mother says Joey is to be pitied because he lost his mother when he was a little kid, and the only way his father ever knew how to deal with him was to give him everything he wanted. But my heart failed to bleed for a kid that had a couple of trail bikes, a motorboat, a secondhand MG, a poolroom in his house, and good looks. I should be so deprived.

I had to stop the car because they were zigzagging in front of me. Finally, Joey Parrish pulled alongside the car.

"Hey, stupid," he said, in his engaging way. "You're going the wrong way. Ball practice is thataway."

"I know," I said, with the bored patience I tried to display to these characters. "I can't go. I called Tom." Tom is the unofficial czar of the team.

"Who you got with ya?" one of the other types yelled.

"A guest," I said, trying to pull myself up like Grandmother. It's hard to pull yourself up when you're jammed in behind the wheel of a car that you're already too tall to be in.

"A guest!" the idiot shrieked. They all began to yell various things.

I gunned my engine.

"I'll take over for ya, Charlie," Parrish yelled.

Great. My only hold on the ball team was that I could throw a fast ball. And I'm a fast runner when I don't trip. But I couldn't hit the side of a barn door, and there was always the chance that I'd be bucked off the team in favor of Parrish, who was at present an outfielder but a good hitter.

As I pulled away, they made elaborate U-turns and headed back to town, making an unholy racket.

"Charles," Lon said, "if you're supposed to be at a ball game . . ."

"Forget it," I said. I felt like a true Christian martyr. "Who cares about it? Let's go out to the cottage, and then to the mill, if you want."

I parked at the head of the lake, and we went over to our boathouse. The lake narrows in, at the end nearest town, with lots of water lilies along the edges. I unlocked the boathouse and we got out the canoe.

"Do you know how to paddle?" I didn't expect he did.

"Yes," he said. "A friend of mine had an outrigger, in Hawaii."

"Well, I don't know about outriggers, but I doubt if they're the same thing. Anyway, take the bow, will you?" I tossed a paddle at him. I was not being gracious.

I was, in fact, being one heck of a boor. But I didn't want to be there, with that person, at that time.

I took the stern, and we started down the lake. It's really a pretty lake, with unexpected coves and one big island and a couple of little ones. It has a lot of forest, right down to the shoreline. In the hurricane of 1938, my grandmother got caught walking from the village to the cottage, and she almost got killed by falling trees. It makes quite a story. I thought of telling Lon about it and decided not to. He was paddling a very decent bow stroke, and we were skimming along okay. The lake was smooth, although it can rough up in a hurry sometimes. One plus for Lon was that he wasn't a chatty type. He didn't say a word after we took off from the shore.

I studied his back. He was so slight, he looked almost like a girl, but he seemed to be strong enough. I wondered if I could beat him at tennis. In Hawaii he'd probably played year-round. And I wasn't such a hot player since I got so tall and ungainly.

A motorboat chugged behind us, and in a minute the Dodge boat passed us. Gerald's older brother Glenn was running it. Glenn was like Gerald, successful at everything. He was president of his class plus star of the Dartmouth basketball team plus on the dean's list. He waved as he went by. I was so busy waving back, I forgot to turn into the wake of his boat. We rocked like mad and almost tipped over.

The Miller cottage is set on a point, and then the lake dips around and goes on for another half mile. Our point is the best spot on the lake because there's almost always a cool breeze, and you have a great view of the mountains.

I guided the canoe into the little cove, which is lined on both sides by cement walls to protect the boats. I caught hold of the iron railing and said, "This is it."

It's a little tricky to get out of a canoe and up the broad cement steps, but Lon did it gracefully, and held the bow while I got out. We pulled the canoe up out of the water. I didn't have to tell him to watch out for scraping the keel.

The cottage is set back a little from the lake in a grove of pine and birch. There's one enormous boulder with a tree growing out of the middle of it. My father remembers when the tree was just a sapling, but now it has split that big granite rock right down the middle. All of us, for several generations back, have had our pictures taken on that rock when we were little kids.

Lon was looking at the cottage. It's an old and very pleasant place, dark brown clapboards, much weathered, with green trim. It kind of fits into the background. The big chimney still had the wire mesh over the top, held down by rocks, that I had put there in the fall to keep red squirrels from going down the chimney and tearing everything up in the cottage.

Lon looked at me. His eyes were that inky black they get when he's moved or whatever. "I have heard so much about this from my father," he said. "He used to draw pictures of it for me." For a kid who was only eight when his father died, he seemed to remember a lot. Maybe some of it was stuff his mother had told him. It's hard to know about that kind of thing.

We walked up the wide porch and I unlocked the door. "It hasn't been opened for the season," I said. "It'll be pretty dank."

I went in ahead of him and pushed back the curtains. The big brick fireplace was blocked up with a piece of heavy cardboard, to keep out some of the cold air that comes down the chimney.

Lon looked all around. He noticed the big hunting and fishing prints that my grandfather had framed in birchbark. I don't approve of stripping bark off birches; they're likely to die. But he did that a long time ago, before people thought of those things.

"I remember those pictures," Lon said, almost under his breath. It was kind of eerie, as if he had really been there before. He walked all around, into the big kitchen with its wood-burning stove; out into the screened-in porch that Uncle Bill and Dad had added for a dining room; into the two bedrooms that were separated from the living room only by what my mother says were called "portieres," heavy, kind of velvety curtains. When I was little, I loved to lie in bed and listen to the grownups in the living room and watch the flicker of lamplight and firelight that showed above the place where the portieres hung by rings from rods.

Lon went up the narrow stairs to the big loft where up to half a dozen people can and sometimes do sleep. He was gone about five minutes and finally came down carrying an old model boat in his hands. I'd forgotten that model was even there, though when I was little, I used to sail it in the cove.

"My father told me about this boat."

I was beginning to think Uncle Bill hadn't done much of anything in Vietnam except spin yarns for his wife and child. Lon put the boat gently on the big oak table and looked it all over. He knew the place as well as I did. I should have given him the key and let him go it alone. I thought of Parrish, probably even wearing my glove, which I'd left at the field, making like the pitcher of the ages. Maybe by tomorrow I wouldn't even be on the team. Parrish replaces Miller.

After Lon had looked at everything about twenty-three times, I said, "Well, let's go over to the mill. If you want to."

"Oh, yes. Is it nearby?"

"Not terribly. We can take the canoe to the far end of the lake and then walk." I locked up.

"What is the name of that mountain, to the south?"

"Tumble-Down-Dick."

"Is it as steep as it looks?"

"I guess. I've never climbed it." I didn't climb mountains; I got too out of breath. I thought I'd probably turn out asthmatic like Dad. "It's some kind of big machismo feat to climb it, usually the day after Memorial Day; that's the tradition." I didn't add that Uncle Bill had been famous for being first to the top.

"I've never climbed a mountain."

I was glad to know there was something he hadn't done.

We paddled around the point and tied up at the far end of the lake, then walked the narrow dirt road to where it crosses the tracks that had been a branch line for the mill. On days when you see hundreds of tiny toads on the tracks, you know it's going to rain soon. I can't say why that is so, but it is; I've seen them there a hundred times and always it rained, even when there hadn't been a storm cloud in sight.

"There isn't much left of the mill, you know. It burned."

"Yes."

The tracks climbed a short, steep hill and hung over the far edge, twisted and bent. One rusty old handcar still sat on top. It wasn't a big hill, but the far side of it had eroded, and you got the feeling you could ride the handcar right off into eternity. The land below the hill was an insubstantial, dark blur of the tops of small trees, scrub oak, and brush. It looked unreal.

We took the path down the easier grade to the mill-pond. The pond was always dark, too, with shadows swinging back and forth over the water. On the other side was the mill wheel, and behind it the dark skeleton of the burned-out mill. Lon stood looking at it all.

"So that's where it all began," he said.

"And ended."

"I don't suppose it will ever end. I mean here we are, whether we like it or not."

It occurred to me that he must feel kind of ambivalent about the Millers. He was half Miller, but his background was Eastern. He must wonder sometimes where he belonged. He'd had to come to us because he had no one else, but I wondered if he hated us. You couldn't tell what went on behind those black eyes.

"The mill and the pond look like a Japanese print," he said, "with that big wheel and everything."

It did. The tall brick chimneys, blackened by soot and weather, shot up into the air, and the lower parts of the brick walls, all that were left, were crumbling now. A few big, blackened timbers lay on the ground with ivy growing over them, and an iron stairway with a concrete base and supports went up the full height of the building that wasn't there and just ended in the air. The whole thing looked as unreal as smoke.

We walked around the pond to the mill. Up close, you could see some rusted machinery lying where it had fallen. The mill had made men's work clothes mostly, and some cheap dress goods. With cheap labor. When John L. Lewis organized the mill workers, my grandfather decided to quit while he was ahead. He didn't need the money anyway.

Lon walked all over the site, pushing aside weeds and ivy and stuff to see everything. You'd think he was going to buy the place.

"It looks as if it had been through a war," he said.

"Do you remember much about the Vietnam war?"

He gave me a funny look. "Of course."

"Well, I thought . . . you were young when you left . . ." I was sorry I'd asked.

"I was eight. That's old enough." He looked up at the stairway. "Do you ever climb this?" He put his foot on the step.

"It's not a good idea. It may have been weakened in the fire."

He didn't pay any attention to me. He climbed up to the little platform that had once intersected the second floor. "Come on up. The view is fantastic."

I didn't want to, but it sounded like a dare. I clenched my teeth and climbed. I get very nervous in high places. By the time I reached the platform and looked down, I had to hang on like mad. My head reeled, and I always get the wild feeling that I'm going to jump. Only I'm not that crazy, fortunately.

"From the top you could dive right into the mill pond," Lon said.

"If you wanted to break your neck."

He gave a strange little laugh. "'. . . for many a time I have been half in love with easeful Death.'" He leaned out so far, I grabbed his arm. "It's like an iron spider's web."

That line from Keats about easeful death startled me. I don't suppose too many fourteen-year-old boys of any nationality go around spouting Keats these days. Even at Country Day, where literature is very big.

Then he gave me an even bigger jolt. "Do you still write poetry?" he said.

Nobody, but nobody, knew I wrote poetry, except the Country Day people who read the little literary magazine I edited, and you could certainly count those people on one-and-a-half hands.

"Who said I wrote poetry?"

"Your mother told my mother. She sent her a copy of one of your poems. It was called 'Alien.' I liked it."

I was furious with my mother, and I was annoyed at his

telling me he liked my poem. Who was he? But most of all, I was astonished that my mother had been in communication with his mother. "I didn't know my mother wrote to yours."

"Yes. Fairly often after my father died. Didn't you know?"

"Nobody ever tells me anything." Until Patty left, I never paid attention to the mail. My father always picked it up at the post office. I suppose Mother didn't tell me because she was afraid I'd tell Grandmother.

"Do you?"

"Do I what?"

"Still write poetry?"

"Of course not." I do. There's a pineapple-shaped knob on one of the posters of my bed that comes off. I keep my poems in the hollow part of the pineapple. Not that my mother is a snoopy type, but somebody might be prowling around. Someday I'll try to get them published, but not till I'm far gone from Miller's Lake.

"That's too bad," Lon said. "I was hoping you'd be a writer."

"Why?" The whole conversation annoyed me. It was none of his business. But I couldn't seem to bring it to an end. I'm always fascinated when somebody is talking about me, even when I don't like what they're saying.

"I thought maybe we could collaborate."

"Collaborate on what?"

"Oh . . ." He looked off across the pond and his voice sounded far away. "About all that happened."

"Well, we could discuss it." I wanted very much to

42

hear about all that had happened to him. Like all writers, I am very nosey about other people's lives.

"If you're not going to write, there's nothing to discuss."

He was so bloody superior. I wanted to make some scathing remark, but right then I had a fit of sneezing. We all sneeze at our house as soon as spring comes, and it goes right on till the first killing frost. I read in a book by Elizabeth Bowen that Romans don't sneeze. That's one more reason to go to Rome, to find out how they manage not to. What if Nero had had a fit of sneezing when he was giving the order to murder Seneca? It might have changed the course of history. A sneezing man is not a man to be taken seriously.

I blew my nose and said, "I'll probably go into the military. Grandmother is trying to get me into West Point." I didn't add that I hated the idea.

He looked at me with real horror. "You wouldn't, would you?"

"Why not? We've always had military men in our family, both sides, right back to the Revolution."

He kept on looking at me as if I'd said I planned to rape, pillage, and plunder . . . And right then it dawned on me that that was what it meant to him. I'm always so busy thinking about what *I* think, I miss what other people are thinking. "It doesn't have to be like that," I said. "An army can work to keep the peace, you know . . ."

But his face was set in a hard line. He had a round face, almost childish and kind of innocent-looking, and when it got this hard look, it was strange, like a child who knew too much.

After quite a long silence he said, "Your grandmother is pushing you into it."

It was odd that he said "your" grandmother. She was his too. "Nobody arranges my life," I said.

He looked at me sideways. "Don't they? Be careful, Charles. She arranged my father's life. As long as she could."

"That's nonsense," I said, sharp and cold. "And I don't think we should sit here criticizing Grandmother, do you?"

He froze. "Certainly not. That wasn't my intention."

"Well, let's split for home. The sun's going down." I swung my leg down and missed the step. I wasn't in danger of falling because I was holding on, but it was scary and not what you'd call graceful. He grabbed my arm. "I'm perfectly all right," I said between my teeth. I found the step and went on down.

We were both very quiet all the way home. I dropped him off at Grandmother's, and when I got home, I was curt to my mother. She looked hurt and puzzled, but I didn't explain. I went to my room, locked the door, and got out that poem. "Alien," from the bedpost. I'd written it after one hot, miserable vacation in New York City with Grandmother.

Alien

Like a surly hoodlum racing down the street,
Pushing me off with the palm of a dirty hand,

New York muttered and roared and hurtled past,
Past me, the baffled uninitiate.
                              And so I came
Home to you again, New England; you
Whom clearer voices than my own have sung
Their songs to, but no greater lovers loved.
And things I had forgotten filled my heart:
Shadows of the elm on the dim white church at
      night,
Moonlight on a broken field of frost,
And crackling chestnuts on an open fire;
Clear, cold, heady air to drink,
In a draft from the tilted jug of autumn night.
And most of all a deep and brooding peace
That deftly weaves my spirit's tattered ends
Into New England pattern once again.

"Crackling chestnuts on an open fire," for pete's sake!
I must have been listening to an old Nat King Cole
record. I put the poem back in the bedpost and lay down
on my bed, trying to imagine what that poem had meant
to a kid like Lon.

4

I TOOK LON TO SCHOOL THE NEXT MORNING AND INTRO-
duced him to the principal, Mr. Ward, and a couple of
teachers and the counselor and my friends, John Pritchett
and Harry North. I let the other kids just stare. Compared to the rest of us, Lon looked quietly elegant in a
gray British tweed jacket, dark flannel slacks, white shirt,
and a tie.

After I left him with the counselor, I didn't see him
again, except the back of his head a couple of times in the
counselor's office. He had to take a bunch of placement
tests and be interviewed and all, and I had a busy day. I
meant to have lunch with him, but Mr. Crane, my English teacher, cornered me and tried to talk me into taking
the editorship of the school paper for next year. I was
very flattered, and I'd have loved to do it; the paper was a
dull bore and it would have been fun to knock it into
shape. But the thing was, I already had a full load of ex-

tracurricular activities. I couldn't give up debating club without a lot of static, and I didn't want to give up baseball because of the effect that would have on my standing. I couldn't tell Mr. Crane that, because it would make me sound very insecure, which, let's face it, I am, but I don't care to broadcast it. I liked Mr. Crane and I wished I could explain to him that in a town where your family is looked up to, it is also looked down on. There was hardly anyone in town who wouldn't have been happy to see a Miller fall on his face. So you have to run like mad just to stay in place. Especially if you're built like a scarecrow and have severe acne. So I said no to Mr. Crane, who was a little miffed.

I saw Lon for a minute after the last bell rang, but I had to go to baseball practice. We still had that Wolfeboro game hanging over us.

In the middle of practice, I looked up and saw Lon sitting in the stands. He looked small and lonely up there by himself. I waved and he waved back.

"Hey, we got a fan," Joey said. He did an elaborate windup. "Shall I drop one on his head? You know, like a bomb?"

I glared at him, and Johnny Pritchett said, "Shut your stupid mouth, Parrish."

Fifteen or twenty minutes later, Gary West got spiked in the knee at home plate and had to be carried off the field and taken home. The coach looked around for somebody to take his place. There were three or four younger kids sitting in the stands now. He looked them over, and then beckoned to Lon.

"Come here a minute, son," he said. And while Lon was climbing down, he said to me, "Does your cousin play ball?"

The situation made me very nervous. "I don't know. I doubt it, coach."

Lon came up to Coach Fuller and waited. He didn't smile, but he was attentive and polite. Coach Fuller clapped him on the shoulder in that hearty way a lot of coaches have, and Lon winced. Joey Parrish laughed. The other guys were watching.

"Do you play ball, son?" Coach said.

"I have played," Lon said, "but I don't like it."

The coach looked shocked. "Don't like it?"

"No."

"We need someone to fill in here for Gary. Can you play outfield?" The coach meant to be pleasant. "Just take off that fancy jacket, and you'll be all set."

Very politely, Lon said, "I'm sorry."

Several of the guys were snickering now, and the coach got kind of red.

"If you're going to school here," Coach said, "it's a good idea to be cooperative, don't you think?"

"I'm sure it is," Lon said. "But I really don't like to play baseball."

"He doesn't know how," Tom Bradford muttered.

"What don't you like about it?" the coach asked him. You could see he couldn't believe his ears.

"I don't like to get hurt," Lon said coolly. "But thank you for asking me." He turned around and walked off the field.

There was a thundering silence. Everybody was shocked. I mean you just don't say right out loud in front of everybody that you're afraid to get hurt.

"Well," the coach said, taking it out on me, "that's quite a cousin you've got there, Miller."

Joey Parrish let out a howl of triumph and all the guys except my two friends joined in. I could have killed Lon. Harry North put his hand on my shoulder and said, "It isn't your fault. You're not responsible for your cousin." But I saw the contempt in the look he gave Lon's retreating back.

Coach hauled one of the young kids into the outfield, and the practice went on; but I took plenty of static, and I was almost sick with rage and shame.

When I got home, I called Lon on the phone and told him to meet me in the meadow. I took my ball, bat, and a couple of gloves. What I had decided was that Lon had never played ball in his life and he hadn't wanted to say so. I got my temper more or less under control, and when he met me in the field, I explained to him that he had embarrassed me very much.

"I'm sorry," he said. "I really am, Charles." But he didn't look to me like a man bent low with remorse.

"I realize you don't know how to play," I said, "but you should have just said so. After all, you're from a different culture. They'd have understood."

He gave me a funny smile. "I grew up in the fiftieth state, you know. They've heard of baseball."

I ignored that, and I gave him a very thorough lesson in how to throw, hit, and catch. He listened. "All right,"

I said, "I'll throw you a few easy ones and you see if you can hit them." I showed him how to stand and how to hold the bat and how to swing. I went out about the right distance for the pitch and I threw a slow ball to him. He hit it. I was so surprised, I almost missed it, but I jumped and caught it just as it was sailing over my head.

"Beginner's luck," I said. "Very good. We'll try another." This time I gave him my speed ball, which is my only real asset to the team. He hit it clear across the meadow into our vegetable garden. It would have been a home run.

"Thank you for the lesson, Charles," he said. He put down the bat and started to walk back toward Grandmother's.

I saw red. I grabbed him by the arm. "Just a minute," I said. "You do know how to play."

"Yes. I never said I didn't."

"Then why the devil didn't you play?"

"I told you. I don't like to get hurt for nothing. I have no desire to be spiked the way that boy was spiked today. I think it's pointless."

I was so angry I could hardly speak. I could feel the tears of anger stinging my eyes. "You disgraced me in front of everybody. You disgraced the family."

He frowned and shook his head. "Charles, this family established this town, didn't they?"

"What's that got to do with anything?"

"The Millers are the first family in the town, as I understand it. Respected, admired, and all that. It is a very strange country, I think, where such a family can be disgraced because a boy refuses to play baseball." He left me standing there.

After a long time I went in for dinner, but I wasn't hungry. I said I had to study for finals, which was true, but I lay on my bed in the dark, trying to think. I felt terrible, and I didn't think I could ever forgive Lon, because I knew he was right and I knew what that made me.

5

WE LOST THE WOLFEBORO GAME, 12–5. I STRUCK OUT three times. I pitched my best, but they had good hitters. It was a disaster. My father said it was just bad luck, which made me feel worse, because I knew it wasn't luck, it was lack of talent. Those guys hit me right out of the park. My mother said it was only a game. That's how much she knows. Mrs. Hancock sent over half a blueberry pie. But when I went over to thank her, I saw Grandmother, and she said I should practice more. She *hates* a loser.

"Sports are a preparation for life, Charles," she said. "If you are careless and slipshod in one, you will be the same in the other."

Grandmother and Lon were just finishing dinner, the two of them facing each other from opposite ends of the long table, like royalty when nobody comes to dinner.

"I have been explaining that to Lon," Grandmother

said. "I think he should become interested in sports. It's an American tradition, after all."

Lon smiled a tight, polite smile. "I am afraid I am just not a competitive person."

Grandmother rapped her spoon on the table. "But all life is competition. If you refuse to compete, you will be stranded in some stagnant backwater."

"Like Albert Schweitzer?" Lon murmured.

Grandmother's head shot up and her blue eyes blazed. "Schweitzer was a genius," she said, "a particular case."

Lon smiled again and bowed his head. He looked perfectly calm but I noticed his left hand, because I happened to be sitting where I could see it. His fingers were clenched around the bottom of the tablecloth, and I had a sudden wild feeling that he was going to snatch the cloth off the table, and all the Haviland china would go crashing to the floor. Of course nothing of the kind happened. Grandmother simply finished her coffee, rose, and left the room.

Lon said, "Shall we play tennis in the morning? It may sharpen my deficient sense of competition."

The next day was a Saturday morning, and we did play. I beat him six-four, six-two, but it wasn't easy. He was a good player; he just didn't work at it hard enough. I am not a great tennis player but I am relentless, and sometimes that wins a game. He didn't seem to mind losing.

"You're a good player," he said. "And you're not nearly as clumsy as you keep saying you are."

Afterward we went to the drugstore and had chocolate ice-cream sodas. There was something nice and decadent about perching on those ancient stools with your elbows resting on the old marble counter, slurping away on a soda at 11:30 A.M. I guess there aren't too many real soda fountains left. We've had this old cluttered drugstore for a million years. It's cool and dim and it smells like vanilla. Lon did his usual thing of taking in every detail. I saw old "Doc," the proprietor, taking him in, too. Doc has owned the drugstore for longer than I can remember. He's a grizzled old guy who never says a whole lot.

Jerry Malone came in for his morning coffee, looking like a slightly soiled dentist in his white button-up coat. He knocked over a box of chocolates from the display. He picked it up, said "hi" to me, shot a look at Lon, and sat down two seats away from him. Doc shoved a cup of coffee at him. He smelled like bay rum.

I saw him sneaking another look at Lon. "Have you met my cousin, Jerry?" I introduced them.

Jerry nodded and mumbled something. After a minute he said, "How do you like it here?"

Lon answered politely that he liked it. Jerry annoyed me. I suppose he isn't really all that bad, but he's snoopy, and Harry North had told me he heard that Jerry made some unpleasant cracks about Grandmother's bringing a slope kid into our midst. I don't know whether he really said it or not; he gets blamed for things other people say sometimes. But I was in a mood to believe it. And I didn't like the way he was looking Lon over, as if he were some kind of freak.

So to bother Jerry, I spoke to Lon in French. All I

said was, "How do you like the ice cream?" And Lon, looking surprised, said, *"Bon."*

But Jerry thought I was talking about him. I knew he would. He scowled and rattled his spoon in his cup. Then he said, "Too bad you lost that game, Charles."

"Yeah," I said. I blew the paper off a straw and it landed in the soapy water that Doc was washing glasses in. He fished it out.

"What you need, Charles," Jerry said, "is to get a drop on that fast ball of yours. Everybody's onto that fast ball. Every team you play is going to belt you right out of the ball park."

"You bet," I said. I paid Doc for the sodas and slid off the stool.

As we were walking to the door, Jerry said, "Remember Pete Bennett, Doc? We had ballplayers in those days."

Pete Bennett was reported missing in action in Vietnam just before the end of the war. He's never been found.

"Remember, Doc?" Jerry raised his voice a little so we'd be sure to hear. "Pete Bennett was the best ballplayer this town ever had. Too damned bad they got him."

I took it as a crack at Lon. "They" meant the Vietnamese.

At the door I said, "Bill Miller was the best ballplayer this town ever had."

Out on the sidewalk Lon looked at me. I suppose I looked mad. "Why do you bother, Charles?" he said. "It's not worth it, is it?"

"What's not worth what?" I said.

He sighed.

I tried to get my temper smoothed down. No point in snapping at Lon. "Jerry is such a jackass."

A couple of freshman girls came along. They giggled and blushed. One of them, Eloise Derby, seemed to have a crush on Lon. I'd seen her passing him notes in study hall and hanging around him in the hall. She was a cute little kid, and since she was a freshman and Lon had been assigned to the sophomore class, that made him an older man. Girls always fall for outsiders, every time. Joey Parrish took Eloise out some, and I mentioned that to Lon, but he just shrugged.

The Friday after Lon and I had played tennis, Eloise invited Lon to the freshman dance. It was the best thing that happened that day. The baseball team dropped another game, this time 10–3. I wasn't the only one on the team who couldn't hit. Anyway, word got around fast about Lon, and I could tell Parrish was burned up. Lon seemed pleased, and he pestered me with questions about what boys wore to dances and what went on and should he send her flowers. I don't think it was so much Eloise, per se, as the idea of being asked. I knew how he felt. I hadn't even gone to my own Junior Prom because I couldn't think of any girl who wouldn't turn me down. At the last dance I went to, I spilled a cup of punch in a lady chaperone's lap. A whole cup. The red kind of punch.

But on the Monday after Lon got the invitation, Eloise cornered me, handed me a note addressed to Lon, burst into tears, and ran. I found him in the kitchen at Grandmother's, talking to Mrs. Hancock. I gave him the note. He opened it with a grin and read it. The grin disappeared.

"What's wrong, dear?" Mrs. Hancock said.

He handed her the note. She read it out loud.

Dear Lon:

My mother says I can't take you to the dance. I hate her. I'm not going to the dance at all. Please forgive me. It's not my fault.

Love,
Eloise

"So that's that." Lon gave us a strained smile and left the room.

I really felt sorry for him. It was humiliating, and it would be all over town by nightfall. I never did like Mrs. Derby. She's a snob with nothing to be snobbish about. She had ambitions for Eloise. Mostly in the direction of Joey Parrish. Joey's old man made a lot of money.

"Can't you do something, Charles?" Mrs. Hancock was feeling bad. She already doted on Lon.

"What can I do?"

"Find him another girl or something?"

"I can't even find girls for myself." But she looked so depressed, I said I'd see what I could do.

I went home and called up John and then Harry, to see if they had any ideas, but they didn't. After all, we're juniors and we don't mess with freshmen. He suggested Tom Cleary's kid sister, and I called her, but she had a date. It was kind of awkward, and I knew Lon wouldn't really like my doing this, so I quit. He'd hate having me beg some girl to take him.

It was of course all over school the next day that Eloise had jilted Lon. She didn't come to school at all. Parrish was all smiles and letting it be known that Eloise had invited him, though I took that with a whole lot of salt. Lon was more aloof than ever, as if the whole thing had never happened.

When I dropped by to report to Mrs. Hancock, in the late afternoon, she began crying. "That slob of a Miriam Derby," she said, mopping her face with her apron. "She's nothing but an ignorant Nova Scotian." Mrs. Hancock always said that the people who lived in Nova Scotia were fine people, but the ones who emigrated to the States were a bunch of bums. That was because her sister's daughter had married a Nova Scotian who had moved to New Hampshire and was a bum. Such is Mrs. Hancock's logic.

"That dear boy," she said. "Have some more pie, Charles. I feel so bad. Such a lovely, sweet boy. People are so cruel. They don't know how children suffer."

"Well, he's not really a child," I said. It was awfully good pie, Boston cream pie, my favorite. It's really a cake, not a pie at all. "And I doubt if he's suffering all that much."

She shook her head and poured me some milk. She knows better than to let me pour it. She tilted her head back, listening. I stopped chewing to listen, too. Lon was playing his ukelele and singing. The sound came very faintly from the wing where his room was.

"See?" I said. "He's all right."

"It's a terrible sad song," she said. Her thin nose quivered.

There was nothing anybody could do about it. I mean, nobody could challenge Mrs. Derby to a duel over the slur to the family honor, or anything like that. I don't know what Grandmother thought of it, or if she thought about it at all. I don't think Lon's life was of the least importance to her, and she probably figured if she was in Mrs. Derby's place, she'd have done the same thing.

"Cheer up," I said. "He'll be all right."

"Your grandmother is so cold with him."

I knew she had to be really concerned, to criticize Grandmother. She always defended Grandmother; they really liked and respected each other.

"I'll keep an eye on him," I said. "He'll be okay."

"Would you, Charles?"

"Sure." I thanked her for the pie and left, without going upstairs. I thought Lon might want to be left alone. When I went by the house below his window, I could hear him singing more clearly. He had a very pleasant voice. Whatever he was singing sounded like a Hawaiian folk song or something, very plaintive. Then the music stopped in the middle of a phrase.

I changed my mind and went back in the house, upstairs to his room. The door was a little bit ajar. I knocked and pushed it open. "Lon? Do you want to go to a show tonight?"

His back had been toward me. He was standing facing a table that stood in the bay window. There were a lot of books on the table. He turned around quickly.

He'd put his uke down and he had a picture in his hands, a picture in a silver frame. I'd seen it before. It was an enlarged snapshot of his mother. Lon was crying.

"What are you busting in here for?" he said. "This is my private room."

I was so amazed I couldn't speak. I'd never heard him speak like that to anyone. But of course I realized what I'd done: blundered in on him when he was missing his mother and crying. I felt terrible.

"I'm sorry, Lon. I really am." I backed out of the room and shut the door. I felt like crying myself. It was an awful thing to have barged in on him like that. All the way home I tried to think what I could do to let him know I was sorry. But I couldn't think of a thing.

6

———

NEITHER OF US EVER REFERRED TO THE INCIDENT. LON WAS his old cheerful self the next time I saw him, and there was nothing I could think of to say that wouldn't make things worse. I just tried to be nicer to him, and spend more time with him.

There was no baseball practice on Wednesday, so I promised to give him a fencing lesson. He came up just as I was getting my foils out of my locker. There were a lot of other kids around, either closing their lockers or just milling around in the hall.

Joey Parrish came along at just the wrong moment, when Eloise Derby had stopped to talk to Lon. Joey had a couple of his goon squad with him. The first thing he did was to bump into Lon. But Lon just stood aside, as if it had been an accident. Of course, me, I began to boil.

Joey had to put on a show to impress Eloise. His back was toward me, so I didn't catch what he said to Lon, but the kids standing close to him looked both scared and pleased, the way people do when they expect a fight. Lon whirled around toward Joey and stepped toward him. He was ablaze with rage. He didn't lay a hand on Joey, but he kept stepping closer to him, all that fury in his face, and Joey kept stepping back, until Joey's back was against the wall right beside me.

In a voice that didn't sound like Lon, he said, "If you ever speak of my mother again, I'll kill you."

There was total silence. I'm sure the other kids felt as I did, that Lon meant it literally. Joey looked scared out of his mind.

Suddenly Mr. Ward was there. "What's going on here?" he said. Although nobody had laid a hand on anybody, it was obvious for a mile around that something was happening. You could feel the electricity.

Nobody answered Mr. Ward.

"Parrish, go to the office," he said.

Joey found his voice. "Listen, Mr. Ward, I didn't do a thing. This guy backed me up against the wall . . ."

"Go to the office," Mr. Ward could sound tough. Joey slunk off down the hall. Mr. Ward looked sternly at Lon. "What was that all about?"

Lon's face was deathly pale and his eyes were very black. He lifted his head and looked straight at Mr. Ward, not a bit like a kid who's been caught out in trouble. In a very quiet voice he said, "He'll have to apologize."

Mr. Ward's eyebrows shot up. "Apologize for what?"

Lon just looked at Mr. Ward.

Mr. Ward reached out to take his arm. "Come on, we'll talk this over in the office."

Lon pulled his arm away as if it had been burned. He and Mr. Ward glared at each other.

"Mr. Ward," Gerald Dodge said. He'd been walking past and seen the whole thing. "It was Parrish's fault. He insulted Lon's mother."

Mr. Ward looked from Gerald to Lon. All the teachers had a lot of respect for Gerald. "Is that true, Lon?"

"He will have to apologize," Lon said again.

Mr. Ward looked a little baffled, as if he hadn't come on this kind of situation too often. Lon just didn't react like the kids he was used to. For one thing, he was obviously not in the least frightened by Mr. Ward or any threats of the office. I wouldn't have been exactly frightened, but I'd have been very nervous.

Finally Mr. Ward said, "I'll have a talk with Parrish. Come to my office before class in the morning, please."

"Please" yet.

Lon nodded and turned away from all of us. Right there I should have said something or done something, but I couldn't think what, so I just stood there like an idiot.

Gerald said, "Wait up, Lon. I'll give you a ride home."

Now all the kids began to jabber. I took my foil and went over to the gym and fought the practice dummy. First I thought of him as Parrish, and then I thought of him as myself.

From the point of view of strategy, it was certainly a lot better that Gerald stood up for Lon than if I had.

But that wasn't the point. The point was, I hadn't. As Marcus Aurelius said, "A wrongdoer is often a man that has left something undone, not always he that has done something." Right on!

7

LON NEVER TALKED ABOUT WHAT WENT ON IN MR. Ward's office, but I got the idea that Parrish had had to apologize, because Lon seemed satisfied, and Parrish struck me as being ready for a vendetta. He kept making pointed remarks at baseball practice. And in school whenever Lon went by, you'd see Parrish and the other Red Flames muttering to each other and making menacing gestures. Maybe they were putting a hex on him. I guess they had to make up for the boredom of their lives somehow.

I tried to warn Lon, but he didn't pay much attention.

"I'd like to see their clubhouse or whatever it is," he said.

So one afternoon when I knew Parrish was somewhere else, we rode our bikes out the old highway. (My father had given Lon his old bike.) It was a pretty road, and a nice spring day. We stopped quite a few times to look at squirrels or spring flowers or just poke around in the woods.

Lon swung from a birch. "I've always wanted to do that," he said. "Ever since I first read Frost."

We came around a curve in that pretty road and there was that ugly, evil-looking place that the Red Flames called their clubhouse. It was an abandoned gas station, with the old pumps still standing out in front. The station itself the guys had painted black, all of it, even the windows. They had skull-and-crossbones painted in white here and there, and over the door red letters said THE RED FLAMES. The paint had run. On the side walls and in back there were obscenities scrawled in white or red paint, as if they had some paint left over and they couldn't bear not to put it to some creative purpose. The door was padlocked, and there was a Red Flames' version of a pirate's flag hanging from the roof, all limp and weather-streaked.

Lon looked at it for some time, and then he laughed. "It's kind of funny, isn't it," he said.

I didn't think so. To me it was evil, ugly, something I didn't like to look at, or even think about. "They're the kind of people that used to turn into Nazis," I said.

He nodded. "Yes, you're right. It's not really funny. It's just that they're so crude and childish about it, it makes you smile."

It didn't make me smile, and I wanted to get out of there. We started pedaling back toward town.

"You're right," Lon said again. "I don't know why it made me laugh. Maybe the way you laugh at the undertaker, because it's so scary you have to pretend it's a joke."

When we came down Main Street, Harold Bumpus came up behind us in his father's pickup and stopped. Harold Bumpus is one of the lesser members of the Red Flames, kind of a pathetic hanger-on. He's got even worse acne than I have, and he's a truly ugly kid. I always thought of him as obnoxious but relatively harmless. Which is probably the way a lot of people think of me.

"Hey, Lon," he yelled. "Got a minute?"

Lon parked his bike and walked over to the truck. He and Harold talked for a few minutes. I couldn't imagine what about. It should have made me uneasy, but it was only old stupid Harold, and the conversation seemed to be friendly.

When Lon came back, he didn't enlighten me. He had a way, a maddening way, in my opinion, of not telling you things. So we went home, and that was that.

One other little thing happened that week. Parrish had seen an old movie in which a Chinese laundryman pulls that ancient wheeze about "No tickee, no shirtee," which, translated, means "If you haven't got your ticket, you don't get your shirt." This and its obvious application appealed tremendously to Parrish's cretin mind. He told the joke all over school, and pretty soon a lot of the kids were calling Lon "Tickee." He didn't know what it meant, so I had the charming duty of telling him. He still looked puzzled.

"But I'm not Chinese. French, English, Vietnamese, and American, but not Chinese."

It was kind of embarrassing to explain that to a lot of ignorant people, anybody born west of San Francisco was the same.

"Oh," he said. "I see. We're all tickees." He shot me an odd look. "I don't suppose it occurs to them to wonder what people west of San Francisco think of them."

It wasn't a subject I really wanted to pursue.

"You know," he said, in a slightly truculent tone, as if it was me that had started all this, "I can't go back to Vietnam, at least not for years, because I am unacceptable there. I am disgraced in my own country because my mother married an American."

That shook me up. I'd never realized that. It was depressing to discover that bigotry was popular everywhere.

"By the way," he said, "I can't go to the movies with you Saturday night. I've got a date."

I was astounded. And consumed with curiosity. But he volunteered nothing. I kept going over in my mind the different girls in town, wondering who it was. Well, all right, Charles, it's none of your blasted business. But I was more than curious; I was envious.

On Saturday night I took my mother to the movies, which set me up as a kind and thoughtful son, although actually I wanted to see who Lon was with. But in vain. He wasn't there at all. The Red Flames were, though, and they kept looking at me and whispering to each other. It made me very nervous. I began to think of that conversation Lon had had with Harold.

After I took my mother home, I got on my bike and

cruised around town, looking for Lon. I didn't want to be obvious about it, in case he was just having an innocent necking party with some girl somewhere, but I was worried. I'd checked, very casually, with Mrs. Hancock, and I knew that she didn't know where he was.

It was about midnight when I decided to give up and go home. After all, I was not my cousin's keeper.

Just as I turned into the gravel road that goes to the Miller houses, there was an ungodly racket behind me. A car, but it had to be the oldest and noisiest car in town. The only one I could think of that sounded like that was the Lightbodys'. I pulled off the road so the old man wouldn't run me down if he was drunk.

But it wasn't the old man. It was Myrtle, and she had somebody with her. She stopped just beyond me, not seeing me, partly because I was in shadow and partly because she was talking up a storm. Her passenger got out. There was a lot of waving and shouting of "good night," and the car lunged off down the road. The passenger started up the road to the Miller place. It was Lon.

8

FOR A MINUTE I WAS TOO STUNNED TO MOVE. THEN I TOOK out after him. I caught up with him near the back door. The light was still on in the kitchen. I grabbed him by the arm.

"Charles," he said.

"Where the hell have you been?"

He gave me a long look that meant it was none of my business. But it was. Everybody was always saying, "Look after Lon, look after Lon."

"You were out with Myrtle Lightbody."

"Yes." He looked amused at my agitation. Amused, for pete's sake!

"Listen." I lowered my voice because I realized I was almost shouting, and they would hear me in the house. "Are you out of your mind?"

"Harold Bumpus asked me to take her out," Lon said. "She wanted to meet me." He smiled. "Not too many people do, you know."

"They were setting you up," I said. "You darned fool. Myrtle is the town tramp. But I guess you know that by now." I glared at him. He had no right to stand there looking so innocent. "Or knew it all along."

"Everyone says she is; she says so herself. So I guess she is. She's a pretty unhappy human being."

"That's one way of putting it." I gritted my teeth, thinking of the story going all over town. "Guess where that slope Miller kid spent Saturday night?" they'd say, grinning at each other. "Out at Myrtle's place." Raucous laughter. If Grandmother ever heard this, it would kill her dead.

"Would you mind letting go of my arm?" Lon said. "I'd like to go in."

"Yes, I'd mind. You're darned right I'd mind. Don't you feel any shame?"

"No," he said. "Should I?"

"Don't you know that you're probably a victim of VD right this minute?" I let go of his arm.

He shook his head. "I don't think so. I think you have to sleep with somebody to get VD."

That stopped me for a minute. What other reason would anybody have for spending the evening with Myrtle Lightbody?

"What did you do, then?"

He began to sound impatient. "Not that it's any of your business, Charles, but we spent the evening rowing around the lake. And if you've ever seen the Lightbodys' rowboat, I think you'll agree that sex would not be practical. For one thing I was too busy bailing." His French accent was very strong, which meant he was mad.

"You could have gone ashore."

"We could have, but we didn't."

"What did you do?" With Myrtle Lightbody what *could* a person do?

"We talked."

"You *talked!*"

"And we sang." He held up his other hand, and I noticed that he had that stupid ukelele with him.

"You're asking me to believe that you spent a whole evening talking to Myrtle Lightbody? The girl is practically a moron."

Now he sounded really sharp. "I didn't ask you to believe anything. And even a moron can have feelings." He stopped me before I could interrupt. "Even a moron, which Myrtle is far from being, even the town tramp, as you all like to call her, can be unhappy. She needed somebody to talk to. So I listened. And then we sang some old songs. It was quite a pleasant evening."

"Lon—"

"I don't care whether you believe me or not, Charles. Nothing could interest me less." He turned his back on me and went into the house.

I walked across the meadow trying to figure out what I thought. It was hard not to believe Lon. In fact, I did believe him. But nobody else would. The story would still go the rounds, just the way the Red Flames had planned it.

And sure enough, there was lots of snickering and

whispering at school on Monday. I was the only one it bothered. Even when Lon was summoned to the principal's office, he was unperturbed. And I had no idea what happened in the office. For all I knew, Mr. Ward may have called him in to talk about grades; but Lon had been getting straight A's in everything. I knew everybody else thought it had to do with Myrtle.

Finally out on the ball field Harold Bumpus came up to me, trying not to laugh, and said, "Miller, just for your own family's sake, you better get Lon to the doctor. He's probably got a disease."

Normally I'd have ignored him; Harold Bumpus is of no more importance than a nearsighted mosquito. But my nerves were on edge and I'd slept badly. So I said, "Shut up, Bumpus. And if you spread dirty talk like that about my cousin, I'll smear you."

He laughed. "Sure you will, Miller. If you don't stub your toe before you catch me."

"You set Lon up," I said. "But he outsmarted you. Nothing happened."

"Ho ho ho." He looked over his shoulder at the other Flames. "'Nothing happened,' it says here." They jeered.

"They spent the evening talking," I said. And of course they yelled with laughter. I would have, too. I sounded like a naive, stupid little kid.

I grabbed for Harold, who is about a foot shorter than I am, but he ducked under my arm and danced away, yelling jibes at me. One of the Flames told the coach I was trying to start a fight with a kid half my size. He bawled me out. When I went home, the Flames followed me on their trail bikes, cutting in front of me and riding in big circles around me. It was a terrible day. I wished that I had never heard of Lon Miller.

9

I HAD JUST COME OUT OF THE POST OFFICE WITH THE MAIL (no letter from Patty) when I heard the Lightbodys' decrepit old car coughing and snorting down the street. I turned and went in the other direction so I wouldn't meet it face-to-face. But there were Parrish and Bumpus coming toward me. I was caught between the devil and the deep blue sea.

I tried to ignore the guys, but Parrish yelled, "Hey, Miller, how's your cousin? Any symptoms yet?"

"Is your grandmother going to send him to reform school?" Bumpus said.

"Knock it off," I said. Which is not a witty or an effective retort.

"Maybe gooks don't get social diseases," Bumpus said to Parrish. "Maybe they're so used to that kind of life, they build up an immunity."

I was going to have to fight these guys, and I didn't

want to. I used to be a fairly good boxer, at Country Day, but now my reactions were thrown all off because of the change in my height. I forgot to compensate for it. But it looked as if I was going to have to defend the family honor whether I wanted to or not. I wished Lon would fight his own battles.

"Listen," I said, "cut out that kind of talk, or I'll . . ."

"You'll what?" Parrish said, grinning.

The Lightbodys' car pulled up right alongside me, and Myrtle got out. The guys forgot about me.

"Hey, Myrtle baby, how ya been?" Parrish went up to her and put his arm around her.

She pulled away from him. "Cut it out, Joey. I'm here on business."

"Naturally," Joey said. He grabbed her long, almost white hair.

Myrtle got mad. She stomped on his foot. He yelled and let go of her. Myrtle is fairly hefty, and if she stomps on you, you'd know you'd been stomped. She's about eighteen years old, I guess, though it's hard to tell. She dropped out of school two or three years ago, still in the eighth grade at the time. She was always having to stay home to sober up her old man. Myrtle had watery light blue eyes and pink eyelids. She looked like an albino, and maybe she was. Her eyeshadow was green, and it had run a little.

"I come to give you this." She held out two dollar bills to Harold Bumpus.

He stared at them. "What's that for?"

"I don't take no money under false pretenses." She

glanced at me. "Oh, hi, Charles. How are you?"

"Fine," I said weakly. I could have cut out right then while the guys had their minds on something besides the Millers, but I was too curious. I had a suspicion of what she was doing, although it hardly seemed possible. Two dollars to the Lightbodys is a whole lot of money.

"I want to tell you you got a fine cousin there, Charles," she said.

Parrish hooted. "Was he real good, Myrt?"

She glared at him. "Lon Miller is a gentleman and a kind person." She stuffed the money into Harold's fist. "That's why I brung back your money. I don't take no money I don't earn."

The two Flames looked at each other. They couldn't believe their ears. Myrtle started to turn away. I saw my chance.

"Myrtle," I said, "you mean, don't you, that you're returning their money that they gave you to seduce Lon, because you didn't do it, right?" I said it kind of loud because I saw Ray Hoffstetter coming along the sidewalk. Ray is the local commander of the American Legion, a friend of Grandmother's. I repeated what I'd said so he'd hear me.

"That's right," Myrtle said. "Them boys paid me to take on your cousin, but I couldn't do a thing like that to that nice young boy. Anyway, he wasn't after anything like that."

"What did you two do?" I said. I could feel that Ray had stopped, in back of me.

Myrtle glanced uneasily at Ray. The respectable ele-

77

ment in town didn't take too kindly to Myrtle, and mostly she stayed outside the town limits. "Why," she said, "I took him around the lake in our leaky boat. We talked a lot, and he played his little banjo, and we sang old-timey songs. He treated me like a lady." She glanced at Ray again. "I got to go now." And to Parrish and Bumpus she said, "You boys, you stay away from me. You just like to make trouble." She climbed into the old car, made a U-turn, and gunned the engine.

I turned around, acting surprised to see Ray. "Oh, hi, Ray," I said. "How've you been?"

Ray was looking hard at Parrish and Bumpus. They took the hint and left. "Those boys give you trouble, Charles?"

"Oh, they tried to cook up a trap for my cousin," I said, "but it didn't work."

"Good." He had a long, narrow head, like a racehorse. The nearest he ever got to a war was Camp Edwards during World War II, but he took the Legion very seriously. "They're troublemakers, those kids. Rodney spoils that boy of his. I guess it's hard, without the mother, but he ought to be stricter. No boy is a bad boy, but they got to be curbed."

I was feeling so triumphant, I probably sounded cocky. But Ray wouldn't have objected to that; he'd have expected it from the Millers. "I guess we can take care of them all right," I said.

"Sure you can. Remember me to your grandmother." He started along and then stopped. "Oh, and Charles, if I can help in any way with that West Point appointment, I'll be glad to. It would be a real honor for the town if you made it."

"Thanks, Ray. I appreciate that." But I wasn't thinking about West Point. I was thinking about Parrish and Bumpus, slinking off in defeat. How sweet it was.

But when I got to Grandmother's, all that euphoria flopped. Mrs. Hancock waylaid me. "She wants to see you," she said, in a voice of dire warning.

"Has she heard about Lon?" I knew without asking that the Hancocks would have known all about it.

"Some woman called up and told her. Said he was doing sinful things. Said he wasn't fit to associate with her kids." Mrs. Hancock's face was dark with rage and indignation. "That sweet, good boy . . ."

"Who was it that called?"

"She wouldn't say. I listened in on the kitchen phone." Mrs. Hancock is nothing if not honest. "Tried to place her voice, but I think she was disguising it. It was a real insulting woman. I can narrow it down to half a dozen . . ."

I'd seen Dr. Adams' car in the yard. "Grandmother didn't have an attack or anything?"

"No, the doc's here to see Lon."

"Lon?"

"You'd better go in. She's in the library waiting for you."

Yes, she was, all right. Standing up, which is always a bad sign. Her back to all those books of Grandfather's on politics and government and mill management. Her mouth was set in that line that means trouble.

"Why didn't you stop it?" she said, not bothering about greeting me.

"I didn't know about it."

"It's your business to know. I asked you to look after him."

"Grandmother, I can't be with him every minute."

"It was your duty to see that such things didn't happen."

I couldn't quite see that, but I decided to try a different tack. "Nothing happened at all, Grandmother. I was just downtown and Myrtle Lightbody came and gave back the money that those kids had paid her to take Lon out."

"You believed that dreadful girl?"

"She gave back the two dollars because she said she didn't earn it. When Myrtle Lightbody gives up two dollars, I believe her, yes."

"He admits he was with her."

"Riding around the lake in a rowboat." But I realized as I said it that it would be almost as hard for Grandmother to forgive Lon for spending an evening with Myrtle, even if they'd done nothing but sing hymns, as it would have been if something had really happened. A Miller having a date with a Lightbody? Poor Grandmother. From her point of view it was total disgrace.

Dr. Adams came into the room. He is very tall and thin, with a walrus moustache that he's had since long before other people started growing moustaches. He's been our doctor since the beginning of time.

"Hortense," he said to my grandmother, in his deep, hoarse voice, "there's nothing wrong with that lad. Not a thing in the world."

"You talked to him plainly, Francis? Did you explain the danger . . ."

I shuddered, thinking of the insult to Lon's dignity. Although Dr. Adams could do it tactfully if anyone could.

"Don't cross-examine me, Hortense, as to my methods of practice. That boy never touched that girl, except to help her in and out of that rickety old boat."

Grandmother closed her eyes for a second, the way she does when the horror of the world is too much. I could see her picturing Lon taking Myrtle by the hand.

"That's a fine boy, that Lon," Dr. Adams said. "Why don't you give him a break, Hortense?"

Grandmother's eyes flew open. "What do you mean?" Even Dr. Adams couldn't be too free with criticism.

Dr. Adams caught the ice in her tone and shrugged. "He's had some terrible experiences for a kid his age. He keeps it all bottled up, and I guess that's very brave, but it's the kind of bravery that can tear a person to pieces in time." He picked up his black bag, nodded, and left.

Grandmother sat down. She stared at her hands, turning her big diamond ring around and around on her finger. I noticed the ring was loose. She'd gotten thinner, and I hadn't noticed.

"I'd be a fool," she said, as if she was talking to herself, "not to know that times change, that the things people experience nowadays are often different . . ." She lifted her head and looked at me, her eyes very blue and intense. "But I have lived my life in the belief that there are certain truths, certain standards, that do not change. I cannot give up that belief now."

She seemed to expect me to say something. I guess it was the time for me to tell her that I didn't want to go to West Point, that I wanted to be a writer, but I didn't have the nerve. I stood there feeling like a rotten coward and a hypocrite. Finally I said, "Lon is a very good kid, Grandmother. He really is. By your standards."

She shook her head. "I don't understand him. He is polite and clean and he does his schoolwork well. But he is as far away from me as the planets. I cannot accept who he is, who his mother was. I may be wrong."

I had never heard her say she might be wrong. It moved me very much. I wanted to hug her, but she had never liked that, even when I was little. Being demonstrative, as far as she was concerned, was some kind of sloppy weakness. It was the time for me to make a restrained but eloquent speech.

I said, "Well, I guess we all just have to . . . uh . . ." She waited to hear what it was we all had to . . . uh . . . But I couldn't think of another thing. Me, the president of the debating team. "Well, don't worry, Grandmother. Everything will turn out all right."

She gave a little shudder. "That's what your grandfather used to say, as he poured another glass of bourbon."

I'd never heard her refer to Grandfather's drinking problem before, either. It occurred to me that she'd had problems I hadn't even thought about.

She got up, and I couldn't help thinking what a disappointment we all were to her. "On your way out,

Charles, will you please ask Mrs. Hancock to take Lon's dinner to him on a tray?"

I couldn't tell whether she was making a gesture of kindness, after Lon's humiliating scene with Dr. Adams, or whether she couldn't stand to face him. I delivered the message and went home.

10

AFTER DINNER, WHILE MY FATHER WAS BANGING AROUND in his workshop, my mother and I went into the living room to have coffee. I'd developed a passion for black coffee. My mother didn't approve, but she'd become reconciled. As I'd pointed out to her, with a little luck it might stunt my growth.

"Do you think Dad would let me borrow the pickup for about an hour, over the weekend?"

She looked surprised. "What do you want that thing for?" Our pickup is a 1951 model and its top speed is 30 miles an hour downhill on a sunny day with a brisk tail-wind.

"Oh, I just need it for about an hour." What I wanted it for was, Johnny Bullock, a friend of mine at Country Day, had written me about a cure he'd heard of for acne. He said he'd heard that if you drove on a dusty road in an open car and got your face good and dusty, and then lay in the hot sun for a while, it would cure acne. Something about a chemical reaction of the dust and the sun. I was ready to believe or anyway to try anything, even a Black Mass if they'd promise me a cure. I wondered if there was anything in literature about a man selling his soul for a clear skin.

"What really happened with Lon and the Lightbody girl?" my mother said. She was shoving her needle in and out on a piece of needlepoint, and she didn't look at me.

"They went for a boat ride. Lon felt sorry for her."

She nodded. "That's about what I thought." She was silent for a few minutes, flashing that old needle in and out. Finally she said, "This is not a town where pity is understood." Flash, flash, went the needle. Then she said, almost under her breath, " 'Were you there when they crucified my Lord?' "

I was amazed. My mother isn't given to flights of imagination. It seemed like a melodramatic quote, and melodramatic she isn't. But the more I thought about it, the more I agreed with her. Christ wouldn't have stood a chance in Miller's Lake.

"And who is more guilty than we are?" she said. "We do nothing to help that boy." She looked up at me almost fiercely. "We're all so afraid of your grandmother. I am sickened by my own cowardice."

"Oh, Mother," I said, "it wouldn't help . . ."

"Of course it would help." She put down her needlepoint. "Call Mrs. Hancock, dear, and tell her we'd like to have Lon come for dinner tomorrow." And she added, "They ask for bread, and we give them a stone."

That didn't seem like the right analogy; more like, they ask for a little affection and we give them bread. But who am I to rewrite the Bible, if that's where it's from. I called Mrs. Hancock.

She sounded pleased. "He'll be glad, Charles. He's been feeling kind of blue. I'll go right up and tell him."

So he came the next night, and all through dinner we were terribly kind and polite, and he was terribly polite and distant.

I kept thinking I'd talk to him and let him know I was with him, but Lon doesn't give you many openings for that kind of conversation. So I showed him my coin collection, and he promised me some Vietnamese coins.

My father started telling Lon about Memorial Day, about the parade and all. I wanted to stop him. I didn't think Lon would like all that martial stuff.

"And Mr. Hancock plays in the Fife and Drum Corps," my father said, "when your grandmother can spare him."

Lon smiled. "Does he play fife or drum?"

"Fife."

"I like the Hancocks very much." It was quite a spontaneous remark for Lon, who usually seemed to consider his statements carefully before he made them.

"They are the salt of the earth," my mother said.

My father wanted to go on about the parade. "The school band plays . . ."

"Off key," I said.

"And the Legion and the VFW march. . ." When my father gets started, he really rattles on. Later sometimes it occurs to him that he's been tactless. "There's a reviewing stand where your grandmother will be because she's a Gold Star mother . . ."

"And because she's Mrs. Miller," my mother said.

My father looked at her. She had interrupted his flow of conversation. He didn't mind; he was just thrown off.

"Your mother sat on the reviewing stand when I was a little girl," my mother said.

"That's right. I believe she did. It must have been because it's named for Grandfather, the Legion post, I mean."

Lon had been listening politely, but the conversation hit a snag.

My father looked at his watch and brightened. "Say, why don't we watch the ball game?"

I groaned. My father thinks it shows he's a red-blooded American if he watches sports on TV.

"We never had a television set. It made my mother's head hurt," Lon said.

In a respectful voice my father said, "What did your mother die of, Lon? We never knew."

Lon looked at the floor. "She died of the war."

"I didn't mean to pry."

"You didn't. She was struck in the back by gunfire, in a village where my aunt lived. The medics took care of her, and when my father came, he took her to the hospital." He paused and spoke carefully. "It healed, but later she developed cancer."

"Oh, Lon." My mother's eyes filled with tears. Then before anybody could say anything else, she jumped up and said, "Would you like to play a crazy card game that the three of us play sometimes? It's really solitaire, but when you play it with several people, it gets really wild. Charles, why don't you put up the two card tables, end to end. We've never tried it with four."

Lon looked as if he would like to get out of it, but I knew my mother was trying to get his mind off his troubles and make him feel at home with us. It seemed like a good try. I got the card tables and four decks of cards.

Lon knew how to play solitaire, but he'd never played it like this. As my mother said, we do get wild. We stand up and yell and slam down cards as if there was a million-dollar pot. In spite of himself Lon got drawn into the spirit of it. For more than an hour we played like maniacs, and I could see he was really enjoying it, especially all the laughing we do. My father was playing up to the occasion, slamming cards on the center aces with both hands and bellowing like a bull when one of us beat him out.

Finally we paused to get our breath, and my mother said, "Charlie, make us some of your popcorn." To Lon she said, "Your Uncle Charlie has a particular talent that shines out above all others; he can make the best, the butteriest, the most delicious popcorn in New Hampshire. It's why I married him."

I saw Lon looked pleased at "your Uncle Charlie," and I realized that he mostly avoided calling my parents anything.

He called after Dad. "Uncle Charlie, do you need any help?"

"No, son," Dad said. "You just help your aunt sort out that mess of cards. And no palming any aces, mind."

I made fresh coffee, and we ate popcorn and drank coffee and Lon and Dad sang some duets. Lon looked up in surprise when the clock struck twelve.

"I had no idea it was so late," he said. "I'd better go." Then he absolutely flabbergasted me. He came around the table and kissed my mother on the cheek. "I've had a wonderful time. Thank you, Aunt Mildred."

My mother's eyes shone when she looked at him, and I thought "She really loves him, not just because he's an orphan." But she only said, "It's much more fun with four. Come often."

I walked him across the fields. We talked about the brook and how high it gets sometimes. I told him I used to skate on it when I was little and had double-runners.

I left him at the kitchen door, and he said, "Thanks a lot, Charles. You people are fabulous."

On the way back I thought about his mother getting shot like that. I wondered if he had seen it happen. What a rotten thing.

11

WHEN MEMORIAL DAY FINALLY CAME, A LOT OF PEOPLE IN town, including the Millers, were usually almost too tired to go through with it. The parade was in the morning, and in the afternoon the Millers traditionally held open house at the cottage. So for weeks my mother and Mrs. Hancock and some of the churchwomen baked beans, made pies and cakes, cleaned up the cottage, and did a million little things. Dad and Mrs. Hancock cleaned the barbecues and made preparations for a huge fish chowder.

It was my job to scrape and caulk and paint the two rowboats, help Dad and Mr. H. get the float into the lake, check out the canoe (which I'd already done), set up the iron stakes for quoits and horseshoes. Et cetera ad infinitum. Lon helped me at my jobs. He couldn't seem to picture just what was going to take place. I told him theoretically the whole town was invited, and a whole lot of them came. The two cottages on either side of us,

Gerald's family's place and the Hardwick place, were also opened up to help with the overflow.

We were all up late the night before Memorial Day, getting the last-minute things done, like laying the briquettes in the barbecues, and stuff like that. We were really tired. But we had to show up early the next morning to go with Grandmother to the cemetery. The Millers had their own little cemetery, as New Hampshire people used to do. It was down near the lake.

Mr. Hancock drove Mother and Grandmother and Mrs. Hancock, and Lon came with Dad and me and the flowers. I didn't know Lon had been to the graveyard, but it turned out he had; Mr. Hancock had taken him, soon after he came.

We all piled out of the cars and went in through the black iron gate. It's kind of a pretty graveyard, with a lot of birch trees. It slopes down toward the lake a little, and you can see the water through the trees. It had rained the night before, and the morning smelled wonderful.

Grandmother took the flowers from Dad and Mr. H. and put them on the various graves, starting with the earliest Miller, whose name was William Charles, born 1740, died 1778. He'd fought with the Green Mountain Boys. Alonzo, his only son, came next. Then Charles Henry and his son, Henry, who was a drummer boy in the Civil War. Then William Charles, a captain in the infantry in World War I.

Grandmother was like a woman at a flower show, businesslike and professional. I was flitting back and forth filling containers with water, straightening the ones that winter and kids had knocked over. My father, in a low, cemetery voice, was telling Lon who the various people were. Lon listened intently.

Then we moved over to Grandfather's grave. He had the most impressive granite monument in the place; he'd picked it out himself and had it engraved. It always gave me a funny feeling to see Grandmother's name on it, beneath his, the date of death left vacant. It was hard to believe she'd be here too.

"Your grandfather," my father went on to Lon, like a guide in a cathedral, "was a major in World War Two. He was a tank commander, with General Patton in the big push across France."

Then there we were at the small headstone that marked Uncle Bill's grave. Like Grandfather's and Great-Grandfather's, it had a small iron cross beside the stone.

My father stopped talking. Grandmother's mouth tightened, and she took a long time arranging the flowers. There were big sprays of purple lilac for Uncle Bill, plus the more permanent geranium plants. Lon held the container steady for her when it began to tip under the weight of the lilac branches. His mouth too was tense, and I thought that really he and Grandmother were a lot alike.

We left at last. Dad dropped off Lon and me downtown, and we went to Sarah's Spa for a cup of coffee. Sarah had just opened up for the summer crowd, and a few early comers were already milling around buying film and the *New York Times* and mosquito repellent. One of the guys, whom I knew slightly, stared at me and then said, "Charles Miller! How are you?" He looked up at me and whistled. "How's the weather up there?"

That is a remark that I'd been trying for a long time to find a witty and crushing retort to, but I hadn't come up with anything. "Fine," was what I said.

We settled into a booth, and Sarah brought us coffee and stopped to talk. Sarah is one of the best people I know. She seemed to have taken a shine to Lon. Outside in the street, Dickie Poole, who was a dairy farmer by day and our police chief at night and on demand, was setting up NO PARKING signs along the parade route. You could hear some of the Legionnaires adding the last few nails to the reviewing stand, and Buster French went by carrying the three flags, U.S., New Hampshire, and Legion, that would flap in the breeze behind the chairs on the stand.

Kids in band uniforms were milling around, and the Legion and VFW men were beginning to show up in their uniforms, complete with Good Conduct Medals. The balloon man went by, and a few minutes later the hot dog man, pushing his cart.

Lon stirred his coffee thoughtfully. "The Millers really have a warrior tradition, don't they."

I don't know why I felt I had to defend them. "Well, I guess it was different in the old days."

He shook his head. "How could war ever be different?"

"Well, you know, fighting for country and honor and all that."

"Honor. That's a funny word."

"I guess it means different things to different people."

" 'Peace with honor,' " he said. "Peace *is* honor."

"I don't know. I think there might be holes in that argument." But I could see he wasn't interested in an argument. He was upset. "You're not going to like the parade and all that, but it's soon over and the party at the cottage is usually kind of fun. We can swim and eat and everything."

He didn't seem too cheered up at the thought.

When we left the Spa, the crowd was beginning to gather. Kids raced up and down the street, the Fife and Drum Corps was assembling, and the bands. Orval Jones, in his Legion uniform, was selling programs that had been run off on the school's ditto machine.

Lon and I sat down on the curbstone opposite the reviewing stand. Pretty soon people were bunched in back of us. An open car draped in red, white, and blue bunting cruised slowly down the street, driven by Ralph Deschamps in his old Army uniform that he could only just buckle over his stomach. The veterans who were too old and sick to march would ride in that car. Some little kids yelled, "Hey, Ralphie!" but he looked neither to right nor to left. Ralphie owned the fish market, and he took his annual Memorial Day chore very seriously.

Gerald and Glenn came along, in white shorts and T-shirts, carrying tennis rackets. Glenn had on a white duck hat with a Roman-striped silk band around it, and he had an unlit pipe in his mouth. They stopped, and Gerald introduced Glenn to Lon. At least in one quarter my cousin was a hero. Glenn began talking about Dartmouth and about Winter Carnival.

Lon seemed to have read a lot about America, and was handling his end of the conversation very well. So I went off to get us some hot dogs from the guy down on the corner with the cart.

I got four with everything. On the way back, pushing through the crowd, I happened to hear two housewife-types, Mrs. George Thaxter and Mrs. Bernie Muldoon, engaged in a conversation about Lon. Naturally I stopped to eavesdrop.

"Would you think she'd have the nerve to let him show his face," Mrs. Muldoon was saying. "That Korean kid of the Millers."

"Vietnamese," Mrs. Thaxter said. "That's a silk shirt he's got on. I never saw a kid his age in a silk shirt. Blue, at that."

"Korean, Vietnamese, it's all the same," Mrs. Muldoon said, "My sister Annie's boy Oscar was over there. He says they're all alike. Shoot first and ask afterward, Oscar says. If you don't want to get it in the back."

"Fragging," Mrs. Thaxter said.

"What?"

"Fragging is what they call it when the gooks shoot you in the back."

You could hear the band starting up, down at the end of the street by the lake. They were playing "The Stars and Stripes Forever."

"It must stick in the old lady's craw," Mrs. Muldoon said with a giggle. "Her and her high-and-mighty ways. The Millers. My Bernie works his fingers to the bone in their garden, and you think they appreciate him?"

"Good morning, ladies," I said, loud enough for the people near us to hear me. Both of them turned around as if they'd been stabbed. Their mouths gaped open. "I heard you speak of my cousin, Lon," I said, in my most cheerful and pleasant voice. "He left Vietnam, you know, when he was eight, but before that time he had a very interesting life. Worked for the CIA, you know."

Mrs. Muldoon opened her mouth but nothing came out.

"In fact, he was a double agent for a while, because he kept getting confused about who was north and who was south. You know how all those people look alike. So he just set up his little tent on the Ho Chi Minh Trail —you remember old Ho—and he sold secrets the way American kids sell lemonade." Behind me somebody laughed. "He was very brave," I said. "Got the Iron Cross, the Croix de Guerre, and three Good Conduct Medals." Several people laughed. "The Green Berets wanted him, but the cap kept slipping down over his eyes."

Mrs. Thaxter gave me an embarrassed little smile. "I think Charles is kidding us," she said to Mrs. Muldoon, whose mouth was still open. Mrs. Muldoon's husband worked part time for Mr. Hancock when he needed an extra hand at Grandmother's. You could read her mind.

"Kidding?" I said. "*Au contraire.*" *Boom, boom, boom* went the drums as the parade came up the street. "You will excuse me," I said. And I plunged through the crowd, holding the four hot dogs aloft like flags.

Just as I got to Lon, Glenn, and Gerald, I stubbed my toe. Two of the hot dogs flew into a mud puddle and a blob of catsup splashed on Glenn's white tennis shoe.

"Oh, lord," I said. Catsup, mustard, and piccalilli streamed into my sleeves.

Glenn laughed and touched the muddy hot dogs with his toe. "Ralph Nader would say it was a fitting end."

A big, shaggy dog pushed by me and swallowed the hot dogs in two gulps. I gave him the other two.

"Hey, that's cruelty to dumb animals," Gerald said.

They were being nice to Lon's clumsy cousin, trying to laugh it off, but I felt terrible. "Listen, my mother has some good cleaner for white shoes," I said. "If you'll let me try it . . ."

"Don't be a dope, man. It'll all come out in the wash." He was just the same height as I was, but on him it looked good. "I'll tell people I shot myself in the foot because Gerry beat me at tennis."

Across the street my father helped Grandmother up into the reviewing stand. The chairman of selectmen sat on one side of her and on the other side was Ray Hoffstetter and Perry Haskell, head of the VFW. There were three other Gold Star mothers, dating from World War II and Korea.

The band was loud now, *oompa oompa oompa*. Marching in front of them came the Legion, out of step but trying. As the flag passed us, the staff jutting out from Tom Terry's fat stomach, everybody clutched at his heart and looked solemn.

12

I DON'T HAVE A VERY GOOD MEMORY OF THAT MEMORIAL
Day picnic as a whole, but certain incidents stand out very
vividly. Like Jerry Malone's youngest kid fell out of the
rowboat, and I had to dive in, in my new white Levi's,
and fish her out. And she was mad at me for saving her.
The kid's got a sharp brain on her, just like her old man.

I remember the Flames didn't actually come to the
picnic, but they buzzed around the area like a bunch of
pesky yellow jackets all afternoon. I found a piece of
dirty paper tacked to a tree out near the archery target;
it said, GOOK, GO HOME. I tore it up fast.

I remember Grandmother sitting in her usual rocking
chair on the porch, overseeing the show, and I remember
the look on her face when the Barber kid challenged
Lon to swim out to the float and back four times, and
Lon was ahead but in the last lap he laughed and cut
around in a big circle. The Barber kid won, of course,

no contest, but no satisfaction either, and Grandmother looked very annoyed. It struck me that there was a clash of cultures here; if you believed in competition, as Grandmother certainly did, then it was bad manners, even contemptuous, to throw a race like that. I don't believe Lon would have seen it that way. To him all this teeth-clenching and grim struggling was childish. Swim because it's fun, that's all. I was torn between the two. I'd have been mad if anybody had thrown a race with me, and yet it *was* silly.

Vivid in my mind is my father's red face as he hung over the barbecue grill, saying cheerfully, "What's your pleasure?" and dishing out hamburgers, hot dogs, and baked beans to what must have seemed like 10 million people. My mother rushed around with a smear of corn relish on her chin, which must have gotten there by levitation, because I swear she never stopped working long enough to eat.

And I remember Mrs. Dodge, Glenn's and Gerald's mother, in her wheelchair that she's been in for five years because of a car crash, looking beautiful and gracious. Her husband and the boys took turns looking after her, and you could tell they thought it was a privilege. That's how Mrs. Dodge affects people. Although my mother, who is seldom critical, once stunned me by saying she couldn't take all that Dodge charm.

I remember Mrs. Thaxter waylaying me tearfully to apologize for gossiping about Lon. "I don't know what got into us. I do apologize, Charles."

I didn't know what to say, not wanting to say it was

okay when it wasn't, so I said, "Well . . ." and gave her a sickly grin. I tried to get away, but she grabbed my sleeve and said, "I don't care what anybody says, Mrs. Miller is good. When Pa came down with the pleurisy and couldn't work at the mill, Mrs. Miller had a ton of coal delivered at our house. And it was her looked after the needy when the mill shut down."

This was getting awkward. I tried to get away, but she wouldn't quit now that she was wound up on the subject of Grandmother as benefactress.

"And look at them, shoveling in the food you folks hand out every year. It's a sin to say mean things about the Millers . . ."

I disengaged her hand. And it wasn't easy. "I'm glad you feel like that, Mrs. Thaxter. Thanks a lot. My dad is sending up distress signals; he needs more hamburger buns." I gave her my wide, false smile and fled. Personally I'd rather take abuse than fulsome praise. Although I suppose at the moment, with her stomach full, she meant it.

The thing I remember most, and always will, about that picnic was Lon's singing. In the evening, when a lot of people had already left, my father built a bonfire down on the sandy beach, and the kids toasted marshmallows. Grandmother was still on the porch with Mrs. Hancock, but I knew she would leave soon. These things tired her, and she never enjoyed them. She was not a hobnobber.

Glenn wheeled his mother near the beach, and I got her a cup of coffee. She told me she'd been talking to Lon about Hawaii and she thought he was charming. I was pleased, though not as pleased as if she'd thought it was me that was charming. But let us be realistic.

Across the lake the sky was pink from the last of the sunset, and the water was inky black except where a breeze made little silvery shivers as quick and flashing as a waterbug's trail.

My father got out his banjo and sang some requests, old-timey songs like "Moonlight Bay" and "Sweetheart of Sigma Chi." Grandmother usually left at this point, but when I looked, she was still there.

Dad got Dickie Poole and some of the others to join in on a song or two. Some people, especially those with kids, left, and the crowd thinned down. The pink was gone from the sky and the stars were sparkling away like mad, almost close enough to grab a few. My father said, "I have a surprise for you. A talented young man is going to sing you a few songs." He made an M.C. kind of gesture. "My nephew, Lon Miller."

There was a smattering of applause, mostly from the Dodges. I didn't know whether I was supposed to join in or not, so I gave a couple of feeble flaps with my hands. When Lon appeared in the circle of firelight, holding his ukelele, somebody behind me muttered something. In the dark I wasn't sure who it was and I didn't hear what they said, but I turned my head and glared, just in case it was hostile.

My father was introducing Lon at some length, telling the audience everything they already knew. ". . . brother Bill's son, as you all know"—yeah, Dad— "lived in Hawaii . . . come to stay with us . . . most happy . . ." My father's greatest problem is stopping. Finally somebody, I think it was Tom Terry, said, "Let him sing."

People laughed, to turn it into an acceptable joke, but I thought it was fairly insulting. My father, good-natured to the end, said, "Right on, Tom. Here he is . . . Lon Miller!"

Lon smiled. It was a just-right smile, pleasant but kind of grave, not catering one darned bit to any blasted audience, and yet saying he was glad to sing for them.

A commotion started way at the back of the crowd, somewhere under the trees. But Dickie Poole, who was sitting behind me, melted into the dark so fast you hardly knew he'd gone, and right away the commotion stopped. Lon gave no sign of having noticed it. He was explaining that the song he was going to sing was an old Vietnamese children's song. It was kind of daring, actually, to start off with music that sounded very strange to us, all that weird Oriental sound that we weren't used to. But somehow it worked. For me, anyway, and I knew it did for the Dodges too. It was a very plaintive little song that made you want to bawl when you thought of all the poor little Vietnamese kids who had died or who were so bad off now.

Without waiting for any applause he went right away into a very jolly little Hawaiian song, something about the volcano, kind of a dare to the god of the volcano. That made a big hit, and everybody clapped. He sang a couple more Hawaiian songs, and then he sang some American songs, "Bucket Got a Hole in It!" "The Old Gray Goose Is Dead," and stuff like that. I was surprised he knew so many American folk songs. The audience was right in the palm of his hand. He had a very pleasant voice, but most of all he had style.

He was standing between the low-burning fire and the dark lake, and the glow of the fire lit up his face. I turned to see if Grandmother was impressed, but she had gone.

Mrs. Dodge asked him to sing another Vietnamese song. Mrs. Dodge's own voice, her speaking voice, is like music. I guess her voice is like those actresses my father carries on about, like Katharine Cornell and Lynn Fontanne; he claims they could have read the phone book and made you laugh and cry and turn white at the gills. Well, that was Mrs. D. And I can tell you this: if she'd ever paid half as much attention to me as she was paying to Lon, I'd have dropped dead with rapture.

Lon sang the Vietnamese song. It sounded very sad, and he looked very sad. I got this feeling that he stood for all the innocent victims of the world's craziness. It made you want to break right down and cry. When he finished, it was very quiet. Then they clapped quite a lot.

"I'd like to sing one more song," Lon said, "one my father taught me when I was a little boy."

I heard this sigh, and I saw my mother sitting near me, tears streaming down her face.

Lon stood with his head tilted back for a moment, his face half in shadow, half lit by the fire. Then he began to sing. I remembered the song right away: I've heard my father sing it. It's an old song called "Down by the Riverside." Lon started it very quietly; behind his voice you could even hear the waves lapping on the shore.

Gonna lay down my burden,
Down by the riverside,
Down by the riverside,
Down by the riverside.
Gonna lay down my burden,
Down by the riverside;
Gonna study war no more.

Then in the second verse—"Gonna lay down my sword and shield . . ."—his voice gradually got stronger. I never knew he had that much power in his voice, and believe me, it shook you right down to rock bottom.

He sang the repeat full strength.

Yes, I'm gonna lay down my sword and shield,
Down by the riverside, down by the riverside, down
*   by the riverside;*
I'm gonna lay down my sword and shield,
Down by the riverside,
And study war no more.

Then he sang the last, high refrain very softly, without the ukelele.

I ain't gonna study war no more,
I ain't gonna study war no more,
I ain't gonna study war no more
Ain't gonna study war no more.
Ain't gonna study war no more,
Ain't gonna study war no more.

The last notes seemed to keep on floating out over the lake for a minute. The waves slapped very gently against the shore, and way back in the woods a whippoorwill called, but otherwise, there was total silence, almost as if people were holding their breath. Mrs. Dodge had her head up and there were tears on her face. Mr. Dodge was holding her hand.

I looked back at Lon, and he was gone. I never saw him go; he just was there one minute and gone the next, as if he had melted into the night.

Finally people got themselves together and gathered up their things and each other and left. I stayed down by the lake a long time, just looking out over the dark water and not really thinking about anything, except I wished I could write a poem about Lon singing that song. But I wasn't good enough.

The moon came up, making a wide silver slash down the lake. I heard my father call me, but I didn't answer. He said, "He's gone, I guess," his voice carrying the way it does across the water. He started the motor, and they put-putted across the water, slicing right through the silver moonlight. I couldn't see whether Lon was in the boat or not.

I took off my clothes, waded into the lake, and swam down the moonlight for a long way. Finally I came back, very cold, dried off, dressed, and started home in the canoe, kneeling in the center and paddling like an Indian. I was a great chief whose mission was to bring peace to all the Indian nations, and even perhaps to the murderous white man. Ain't gonna study war no more, ain't gonna study war no more . . .

13

SOMETIMES YOU GO THROUGH AN EXPERIENCE THAT YOU think ought to change the world and then you find out it hasn't really affected anybody, except maybe for a minute. Lon sang those songs to get a message across. I think it hurt his feelings that all people really got was that he had a pretty voice. It was like Lord Byron dying for Greek independence; who ever thought anything about him except that he was handsome and romantic and club-footed and slept with his sister? People aren't really interested in ideals.

So nothing was changed when school ended, and I went to work at the recreation center in the park giving tennis lessons. It has always been true of me that I don't do things very well myself, but I sure as the world can teach other people how it ought to be done. Result: there are tennis players, baseball players, pitchers, hitters, drivers of cars, and fencers who can beat me at any kind of competition you want to name, whom I taught how to do what they do so well. There's got to be a name for that.

Once I started working, I didn't have time to see much of Lon, but I heard from the family that Mr. Hancock was teaching him to be a gardener. The few times I saw him, on my way home, he was out there in a pair of old white shorts pulling weeds, transplanting, and who knows what.

I heard fragments of a story to the effect that Parrish had challenged Lon and me to climb the mountain the day after Memorial Day and we had chickened out. I was too busy to care about the story, and I couldn't imagine Lon would care. I also heard that Lon was a Red-Communist-Pacifist, I suppose as a result of singing that he'd study war no more. People's stupidity would be laughable if it weren't so serious.

Grandmother took off for her annual spring jaunt to New York, to shop and see some shows and old chums. On the night of the Grange meeting, my mother invited Lon to dinner, because the Hancocks would be at the Grange. But I had to work late, giving a lesson to a couple of kids from Milton, on my own time and for money. So when I got home, it was about quarter to ten, and Lon had gone.

It was a funny night, weather-wise, kind of windy and threatening a thunderstorm, which was why I was so late; I had taken the kids inside for a chalk talk.

I'd just showered when my father called me to the phone. It was Lon, and he sounded kind of strange.

"Why don't you come over?" he said.

"All right. What's up?"

He laughed. " 'I am a stranger and afraid in a world I never made,' " and he hung up.

I sighed. I was tired. But I was also curious. I hauled on my dirty tennis shorts and a clean T-shirt and told my mother where I was going.

"Good," she said. "He seemed bothered about something."

The wind was blowing up a storm as I crossed the meadow, and I saw a couple of flashes of lightning. But the thunder didn't roll till I went in the kitchen door. The phone was ringing, and it kept on ringing, so I picked it up.

"Hello?"

A fake falsetto voice said, "Is this the Miller residence?"

"It was, the last time I checked."

"Lon Miller, please."

"Who's calling?" It sounded like Parrish.

"A friend."

"Yeah? Well, there's no one by that name here." I could tell that stopped him for a minute.

"Who is this? Is this Miller? Which Miller is this?"

"This is the miller that makes the flour that bakes the bread that feeds the army that conquers the world. Any message?"

The receiver clicked.

I slammed down the phone, and there was Lon in the doorway, laughing. "How long has that been going on?"

"Oh, ever since Grandmother went to New York. Before that, I think she got some calls."

"Is that why you're a stranger and afraid, et cetera?"

"Oh, gosh, no. They're just a nuisance, like a horse-fly. No, it's being alone in the house that scares me."

I was amazed. "Why?"

"I'm afraid of the dark."

"You're kidding."

"Not at all. In a house alone at night, with a storm brewing . . ." He shivered. "Come on upstairs and buck me up."

Up in his room, I said, "It's crazy to be afraid of the dark."

"Of course. And I knew you'd say so. But listen." He had a copy of Frost's poems on his desk. He read me the one titled "Bereft."

Where had I heard this wind before
Change like this to a deeper roar?
What would it take my standing there for,
Holding open a restive door,
Looking downhill to a frothy shore?
Summer was past and day was past.
Somber clouds in the west were massed.
Out in the porch's sagging floor
Leaves got up in a coil and hissed,
Blindly struck at my knee and missed.
Something sinister in the tone
Told me my secret must be known:
Word I was in the house alone
Somehow must have gotten abroad,
Word I was in my life alone,
Word I had no one left but God.

For a couple of minutes I didn't say anything. Then I said, "To tell you the truth, I'm not all that crazy about the dark myself."

He smiled and lay on his back on his bed. "How's the tennis?"

"Okay. Pretty boring. How's the gardening?"

"I like it."

His room had become very much his. The picture of his mother was on the desk. I noticed he had a pair of foils; they looked like old ones of mine. There was a picture postcard of Hawaii tacked to the wall. "Where's that? Which island?"

"Hilo. *Hilo no ka oe.*"

"Meaning?"

"Hilo is the best."

I got him to talk about Hawaii. It was pretty interesting. It began to rain; lightning streaked across the trees, but the thunder wasn't very close. We talked about fencing, school, how much water hollyhocks need, and the problems of teaching a southpaw to serve.

The phone rang, but he said, "Don't answer it." It rang for about three minutes, and it got on my nerves. I had an attack of sneezing.

After a while he asked me a question about fencing. I said, "Come out in the hall and I'll show you."

We fenced for a while, and it got pretty lively. We were laughing a lot. I said, "I hereby dub you Warden of the Butteries and Groom of the King's Posset." I laid my foil on his shoulder.

There was a real smash of thunder. "The gods approve!" he said. Then the lights went out, and seconds later someone pounded on the front door.

"I must have locked the Hancocks out." Lon put down his foil on the hall table and ran downstairs.

I followed him. The Hancocks usually came around to the back, but I couldn't think of anyone else it would be. My parents always came to the back because it was nearest our house. But of course it was raining like fury; probably Mrs. H. wanted to dash in out of the rain.

I was standing at the curve in the stairs when Lon opened the front door. The wind caught the door and flung it wide open and the rain poured in, in Lon's face and on the rug. There was nobody there.

"They must have gone around back," I said. "Shut the door, man." The living-room curtains were blowing and a copy of *House Beautiful* flipped its pages.

Lon closed the door. The lights flickered on, just long enough for me to see Lon's face. He looked frightened. Then it was dark again, and someone was pounding at the back door. Now this was strange. I knew the back door was unlocked, because I'd come in that way. Somebody yelled outside. I was almost downstairs when Lon ran down the hall to the back of the house. I called to him to wait for me, but he was already out of sight. I heard him bump into the table at the far end of the hall, and then I heard the creak of the swinging kitchen door. The lights kept coming on and going off again, so you couldn't adjust to the dark, and the rain was beating on the house, trees were cracking and groaning, lightning lit up the outdoors for a second and then the thunder really crashed. The whole thing was like a scene from the *Inferno*.

I hit my shin on the same table Lon had hit. It hurt like sin. As I limped into the kitchen, the lights went on and stayed on. The kitchen was empty. The back door was blowing wildly open and shut, *bang, bang, bang.*

I turned on the outside light and hollered for Lon. No answer. As I went out, I heard something out on the road, a car maybe, and a smaller sound, like a motorbike. I went all around, calling and looking. I ran up and down; I beat the bushes. I was in a panic. I was convinced somebody had killed Lon. Looking back on it now, it seems pretty hysterical, but at the time I was sure. I could imagine the Parrish bunch killing him and calling it patriotism. I could even imagine some of the harpies, like Muldoon, offering him up for sacrifice. Or Jerry Malone, the superpatriot . . .

I came around the corner of the house and saw a word written in big black letters on the white paint, the letters already blurring from the rain. TRAITOR. That was the word.

I didn't even stop for a bike; I just ran. I guess four or five times I slipped in the mud and almost fell flat. When I reached the road, I saw the ruts made by trail bikes and by a small car, like an MG. They were already filling in with rain and dirt. Footprints too, and a big kicked-up place that might have been people struggling. I ran toward town.

It was pitch dark except for the occasional lightning. Once I ran right off the road and crashed into a tree. For a minute I was really groggy, and I could feel the trickle of blood where I'd scratched my forehead. My one idea was to get out to the Flames' place. I was sure that they had taken Lon out there, dead or alive. Maybe they were torturing him.

If I ever ran as fast as I did that night in a ball game, I'd be a sensation. I could hardly breathe by the time I got downtown. I was gasping real loud, and my hay fever was going full blast. Fortunately no one was around, because it was still raining hard. At least I thought no one was around, but after I went by the drugstore and on up the street to the old highway, somebody stepped out of the shadows and grabbed me. I was so surprised I lost what little balance I had left and fell flat in a big puddle.

The guy who helped me up was Dickie Poole. "What's up, Charles?" he said. He steadied me with one hand and with the other mopped my wet and bloody face with his handkerchief. I must have been an awesome sight.

I could hardly talk. "Lon," I said. "Lon . . . kidnapped. Parrish . . ." I couldn't make it beyond that, but he got the point. He hauled me over to his police car, which I hadn't even seen in the dark, and in like twenty seconds we were speeding down the street and out the old road.

He shut off the engine and let the car coast up close to the Flames' clubhouse—although in that downpour they might not have heard us anyway. Dickie said, "Wait," but I was too scared to stop for strategy. I flew out of that car and into the weedy driveway. The Flames' place was dark, but you couldn't see a light from the outside anyway.

I expected the door to be locked, but it wasn't. I gave it a big yank and it opened. I nearly fell over backward. Everybody looked around. It was an eerie scene. The only light was from a couple of candles stuck in bottles, throwing huge shadows on the walls. And what walls! They were covered with pictures of Playboy bunnies, a big picture of Hitler, a swastika, and an American flag.

For a second I couldn't distinguish who was who. Then I saw that Parrish was standing astride Lon, who was flat on his back on the floor, held down by a guy at his shoulders and one at his feet. Lon was struggling, but they had him pinned. Harold Bumpus was standing beside Lon, holding a homemade banner with the Red Flames' pitchfork painted on it. The other guys were just standing there watching.

A couple of them made a dive at me, but I yelled my wildest Comanche yell and dove into them, arms flailing, and I've got long arms to flail. One of them, and I saw it was Tom Terry's kid, sailed over backward, and the Haskell kid stumbled back and fell over a chair. Parrish and Bumpus both jumped for me, and the guys who were holding down Lon let go. Dickie Poole was in the room then, and a bunch of the guys were trying to get out. He got hold of Bumpus and the Terry kid and hauled them off to the police car. He hollered to the others not to move, but most of them got out and disappeared in the dark. The Haskell kid got up and tried to nail me with the chair he'd fallen over. It came crashing down, but I ducked, and Haskell fled just in time to fall into Dickie's arms.

I turned toward Lon. He and Parrish were struggling. Before I could get into it, Lon broke loose and gave Parrish a shove, then jumped after him. For a second I thought I was going to see some karate or kung fu, but Lon just gave Parrish an old-fashioned American sock in the jaw, and it was a dilly. Parrish went over and lay as still as a stone, blood trickling down his chin.

Dickie gave Lon a quick look as he came back in and saw Parrish. Then he slung Parrish over his shoulder like a sack of potatoes.

"You guys get in the car," he said to us. He heaved Parrish into the back seat right on top of Bumpus, Terry, and Haskell. Terry was whimpering like a little kid.

Dickie went back to put out the candles. The rain had stopped, and I could see him inside, looking shadowy and distorted in the wavering candlelight. He ripped down the Hitler poster and the swastika and tore them up.

Nobody said a word all the way to the Town Hall. He shooed us into the police office, which was the only room in the Town Hall with a light on. Parrish was on his feet by that time, but he was groggy and he had a big lump on his jaw. He avoided looking at anybody.

Lon didn't look too great either. He had a nasty cut on his forehead, his black hair was all mussed up, and he was very white. When Dickie gave him a piece of Kleenex to wipe the blood off his hand, he didn't seem to know what it was for. I took it and wrapped it around his knuckles.

Dickie sat down at the desk and got out some forms. He said to Lon, "You want to bring charges?"

Lon shook his head.

Dickie gave him a thoughtful look. Then he said to the Flames, "I'm booking you for disturbing the peace, for starters. You can sit in the drunk cell while I call your folks." He herded them down the hall to the drunk cell, which is the only jail we have.

Lon leaned against Dickie's desk, staring at the floor. He looked kind of sick. Dickie came back and hung up the cell key. "I'll take you home." He drove around to the back door. "The Hancocks won't be home from the Grange yet." He took his black first-aid case and followed us into the kitchen. "Sit down, Lon."

"I'm all right."

"Sit down a minute." He put a little water in a saucepan and turned on the stove.

Lon sat down. Dickie got some gauze and some tape from his case. He carefully lifted Lon's hair and looked at the cut. It was oozy and nasty-looking.

"Does your head ache?"

"No."

Dickie looked at me. "Maybe Doc ought to take a look at it."

"No," Lon said, very firmly. "It isn't necessary."

"What were you hit with?"

"I'm not sure. I was trying to get out of their place. Somebody hit me with a pipe or something."

"Did they hurt you otherwise?" Dickie made it sound more like a casual chat than an investigation.

"No."

"They were standing over you . . ." I began, and then decided it was none of my business.

"They were trying to get me to sign something."

Dickie used the warm water and a piece of gauze to clean Lon's forehead. He was very gentle. "Sign what?"

"Oh, some stupid things about my mother."

I forgot I was going to keep still. "Parrish is hipped on the subject of your mother."

Dickie fitted a gauze pad over the cut and carefully taped it. "Might be because he never had one."

"Never had one?" Lon moved his head quickly.

"Easy. Hold still a sec." Dickie fixed the tape. "His mother died when he was born. Rodney's idea of bringing up a child is always to make sure he's got a pocketful of money. The kid never had much else."

"Not having a mother doesn't excuse him," I said.

"Not excuse. Maybe partly explain." Dickie stood back to look at the bandage. While he was washing up, he said, "I enjoyed your singing out at the lake."

"Thanks." Lon was frowning, worrying about something. When a Miller worries, it sticks out all over him.

"You've got a good voice. Like your dad. Your dad and I used to double-date. Long ago. On the way home with our dates, we'd sing up a storm." He laughed kind of a sad little laugh and dried his hands on a paper towel. "Long time ago." He closed the first-aid kit. "Charles, you better stay here. I'll stop in and tell your folks. Does your grandmother keep whiskey in the house?"

"I think so."

"Give Lon a shot and a couple of aspirin." He waved. "See you."

"Mr. Poole?"

"Yeah, Lon?"

"Do you think I broke Parrish's jaw?"

"No, no. It's just going to hurt for a few days."

"I wish I hadn't done it."

"Sometimes these things happen. Don't worry about it." Dickie left.

I'd been looking forward to telling Grandmother about our grades, which had come right after she left. Both Lon and I had made the honor roll. Now with all this mess, that wouldn't even be noticed.

14

"I WISH I HADN'T DONE IT," LON SAID AGAIN, WHEN I'D
finally talked him into getting to bed, drinking the shot
of bourbon, taking the aspirin.

"There's a limit to how far you can turn the other
cheek," I said, "without your darned head falling off."

"But it's just what I'm against, 'You hit me, I'll hit
you.' It's so bloody stupid and barbaric." He was beginning to sound sleepy.

"Worry about it tomorrow," I said.

"You going to stay here?"

"Sure." In a pair of silk pajamas that his mother had
made, he looked like a little kid. I had this crazy impulse to pat him on the head. Not that I did. I had that
much sense.

"My mother told me," he said, "about the time she
went to England with her father. She was fourteen or
fifteen. They went to Coventry, which was very hard

hit by the Nazi bombs in the Second World War." He lifted himself up on one elbow, not looking sleepy now. "This beautiful old cathedral was bombed. Well, instead of rebuilding it, the English left it the way it was, with two walls standing. They planted grass over the rubble. And where the altar had been, they made a great big cross out of the charred timbers . . ." He stopped and bit his lip. "My mother said that big cross soared right up into the sky. And there's a plaque that says, FATHER, FORGIVE." His voice broke, and he slid down under the covers again, turning his face away. "Good night, Charles."

Well, it had been a busy night. I washed my face with very hot and then very cold water, as was my wont, and then I called my parents to say all was okay. My mother was at her best; she just said, "See that Lon gets a good sleep."

They were also, my parents, at their best a few days later when Dickie called a meeting of the kids and parents involved in what I guess you could call the Flames' Clubhouse Caper. In Miller's Lake everything that happens is instantly known to everyone, and everyone instantly takes sides. I'd say about eighty percent of the town, give or take a few, had opted for Parrish. There he was, after all, parading around town with a swollen jaw. Native son and all that. Maybe a little wild sometimes, but what can you expect without a mother to guide him? And when some foreign kid thinks he can come in here and act like some kind of Chinese peace-nik, and then beat up on one of our boys . . . And after all, his mother . . . And, who does old lady Miller think she is? After all . . .

Old Lady Miller was still in New York, but Charlie Miller and his wife and that stupid boy that's nine feet tall and has a rotten complexion—we were all there. So were most of the parents of the Flames involved, including Rodney Parrish, with his usual cigar. The meeting itself was unconventional. Dickie never does things in a conventional way. People gripe and complain, but they keep on reelecting him because they know he's fair and honest, and most of the time that's what they want.

He called the meeting to order, and then he sat on the edge of his desk and gave a brief account of what he had seen. He asked Lon if that was substantially correct. Lon said, "Yes." He sat between my parents looking pale but composed. Dickie asked Parrish if it was substantially correct. Parrish grunted.

Rodney Parrish stood up. He looked unhappy and said, "Dickie, you haven't gone into the all-important subject of motives."

"No," Dickie said. "Motives are not my business."

"But even in a court of law, Dickie, motives are taken into account."

"This isn't a court of law, Rodney. It's an inquiry into what happened. I'm no psychologist about motives and all."

Rodney looked bewildered and sat down. He makes a lot of money as a contractor, but in other ways he really doesn't seem too bright. Once he ran for chief himself and got like twenty-seven votes.

Dickie ran the inquiry like a small Town Meeting. Whoever wanted to speak up, could. The only trouble with Dickie is he's too nice a guy to be a completely effective law man. He listens to everybody, and sometimes these things really run on and on. Tom Terry held forth for a while about boys will be boys and the long, hot summer. He seemed unhappy, and you could tell he'd had a row with his kid, who sulked and stared at the floor. Tom said the whole thing had just been an initiation ceremony, like.

Harold Bumpus' mother got up. She is a timid soul to start with; she always ducks a little when you speak to her, probably from the long habit of ducking her husband's fist. In a voice you could hardly hear she said she tried to do right by her boy but he'd got in with a rough crowd. Joey Parrish looked up for the first time and laughed out loud. His father gave him a quick cuff on the back of the head. Joey's jaw was still swollen.

Mrs. Bernie Muldoon, who was an aunt of the Haskell kid, said her brother and his wife were in Atlantic City at a VFW convention, so she was there to say no one could ask for a better boy than her nephew George, high-spirited like any good, fun-loving American boy, but certainly not malicious, no indeed, and it was too bad when an outside element crept into a town and caused trouble.

After she sat down, it was quiet for a minute. It was the closest anyone had come to an outright attack on Lon. And I knew what was bugging her. Mr. Hancock had let her husband go when Lon got interested in the gardening. There wasn't enough work for both, and Mr. Muldoon was a sloppy worker.

My father got up and I really tensed. If he got going and couldn't stop . . . And I knew he was nervous because he kept fiddling with the zipper on his jacket pocket. He cleared his throat and smiled his smile of supplication. I closed my eyes.

"Chief Poole," he said, "ladies and gentlemen."

Inside my head I groaned. He sounded like the Rotary Club speaker. "What took place the other evening," he said, "involving my nephew and my son, was the kind of thing I hoped never to see in this town. My friend Tom spoke of it as an initiation." He stopped and swallowed. "In my opinion it was an initiation into bigotry and malice and pure cussedness, and it's got to be stopped before our whole town is infected . . ." His voice broke and he sat down. Lon, on the other side of him, gave him a smile I can only call radiant.

My mother popped up. "Dickie," she said, "and all of you, I would like to agree with my husband and add one more thing. I have never known a more gentlehearted boy than Lon Miller. It would be tragic if—"

She was interrupted by Mrs. Muldoon, who shot up with a face as red as a boiled lobster's. "Miller, Miller, Miller! I'm fed up to here with Millers. They've run this town long enough. What I say is—"

What she had to say was lost to history, because somebody began to boo and then some other people applauded and it was bedlam. Dickie tried to outshout them to get some order, but finally he got disgusted and left the room. Meeting presumably over. People got up, yakked to each other, milled around, left. Lon went over to Joey Parrish, leaned toward him, said something, and put out his hand. Parrish looked surprised, then embarrassed, and he shook hands without looking at Lon. Rodney grabbed Lon's hand and shook it.

When I came out of the hall, this joker who writes for the county weekly tried to question me. I told him to get lost. You don't do that with the press if you're smart, I learned. A week later Grandmother and the newspaper arrived within half an hour of each other, and I'm sure Grandmother was charmed to see a front-page story headlined RUCKUS IN MILLER'S LAKE, with a subheadline that said, "Miller Dynasty Challenged." The guy apparently thought he was the second Mark Twain or something. He wrote up the story, with a million distortions, as if it were the Tudors being challenged by the Stuarts or whatever. I'm sure he thought it was a hilarious piece of social satire. Lon was referred to as the "heir presumptive from over the seas." I was punished by oblivion; I was not mentioned at all except in the last line of the account of the fight, where it said, "Young Charles Miller . . . is this Charles the Third? Sixth? . . . was on the scene long enough to demonstrate the length of his arm and the inaccuracy of his aim, as per baseball." Referring to Grandmother, the story said, "The restraining, or some say the repressive, force, the Dowager Queen, was in New York at the time. We have been unable to reach her for comment, a situation to which the years have accustomed us." That's yellow journalism country style.

The Hancocks scampered to get the paper before Grandmother did, but she had beaten them to it. Lon was summoned to her bedroom, where she was resting. I do not know what went on. But I do know that Lon was terribly depressed about the whole affair, though in my opinion about the wrong things. He felt awful about having made enemies. He still hadn't gotten over socking Parrish. And he felt he had brought sorrow and disgrace to the Millers. I tried to make him see that his father, from what he had told me, had been on just the same kind of collision course with the "respectable" element in town and with Grandmother especially. But Lon was past reason and consoling.

Later in the day Grandmother summoned me. She was still in bed, which was unusual. She looked tired. That stupid paper was on the floor beside the bed, also unusual, since Grandmother would rather be burned at the stake than dump stuff on the floor.

After I had kissed her and inquired about her trip, she said, "Quite a lot seems to have gone on."

"Yes."

"Hancock tells me there is much feeling in the town."

"Oh," I said, "they're always looking for something to get wrought up about."

"I would like to hear your version of what occurred, please. Without embellishments."

I gave her my version, without embellishments. She listened without expression, her eyes closed. When I finished, she said, "Thank you. Please ask Mrs. Hancock to bring me tea and toast."

That was the day Johnny Pritchett said he heard Rodney was going to bring suit against the Millers because of Joey's jaw. I doubted very much if it was true.

"I don't know," Johnny said. "People are laughing over it, anyway. I mean if people sued people every time some kid hit another kid. It's ridiculous."

Whether Rodney had said it or not, he never did it. But it was one of the things that kept the whole stupid story going and that irritated Grandmother more than anything else.

Lon, in the meantime, kept more to himself than ever. He went off nearly every day as soon as he finished with the garden chores, and he stayed away until bedtime. Mrs. Hancock usually fixed him some sandwiches. He borrowed the boathouse key from me. I didn't have time to pay as much attention to him as I wanted. I was too busy teaching lobs and backhands and such.

Then something pleasant happened. Mrs. Dodge invited Lon and me to Sunday dinner at their cottage.

15

THE DODGES REALLY PUT THEMSELVES OUT TO GIVE US A good time, or especially I guess to give Lon a good time. It was the first reason Lon had had to smile for quite a while.

We left the boathouse in the canoe about three o'clock. It was a beautiful, calm day, and the only fly in the ointment—or the only unwelcome fly in the lake—was Jerry Malone and Buck Muldoon, fishing from Jerry's old putt-putt. They circled us and enjoyed making the canoe rock. With a bottle in the stern that I'm sure wasn't full anymore, they were feeling no pain. When we docked at the Dodges', they went past the place a few times and then anchored and fished offshore. I forgot about them finally because I was having too good a time to worry about those drunken oafs.

We swam for a little while and then dressed and helped Gerald and Glenn get the barbecue going. Mr. Dodge cooked fantastic steaks, and Mrs. Dodge had made a marvelous potato salad and fresh asparagus and garlic bread and iced tea. The boys had made strawberry ice cream in the ice-cream freezer.

We ate in their big screened-in front porch and it was really nice. Some day I'm going to screen our porch; then you can sneer at the mosquitoes.

Mrs. Dodge had asked Lon to bring his ukelele. After dinner, and after we guys had done the dishes, Lon sang for a while, and then Mrs. Dodge sang a few songs. She had grown up in Quebec, and she sang some neat French-Canadian folk songs. She had a low, husky voice, not much range but very pleasant.

Thanks to Lon I was getting to really know the Dodges, whom I had always admired and never gotten close to. They were awfully nice to me, although I knew it was because of Lon. At first I was afraid the Flames thing would come up, but I should have known they'd be too tactful for that. They were showing us their support just by having us there.

I really hated to have the day end, but Mrs. Dodge began to look tired. When I said good night, she took my hand and said, "I'm glad we're getting to see more of you, Charles. You've been one of my favorite Miller's Lakers for years." I really went out of there flying high. It wasn't till later that I wondered who her other favorites were.

It was a dark, cool night on the lake. We flew along in the canoe, not talking at all. I hoped Lon had had a good time. He needed one.

When we beached the canoe, I got out first because I

was paddling bow. I steadied the canoe while Lon came up, so he wouldn't get his good shoes wet. We put the canoe in the boathouse and locked up.

I took a couple of steps away from the boathouse and almost stepped on somebody. Lon turned on his flashlight. It was Muldoon, drunk as a skunk (an unkind thing to say about an animal as nice as a skunk) and unable to get up. Jerry Malone emerged from the darkness, drunk but still able to navigate. He was holding a bucket of fish.

"Evening, gentlemen," he said, with that silly giggle some drunks get. "Have a nice day?"

"Sure, Jerry." I certainly didn't want to tangle with him. Although he really didn't seem belligerent, just smashed and silly. I stepped past him and then waited for Lon to catch up, with the flashlight.

Jerry started to say something to Lon, but he staggered and lost his balance. He grabbed at Lon's arm in a kind of falling-down motion and knocked the ukelele out of Lon's hand. Lon made a wild reach for it, but it fell on a sharp chunk of granite and splintered. Lon groaned, a quiet groan that was worse to hear than a scream. He picked up the pieces and stood looking at them in the dark. He had dropped the flashlight. I got it and turned it on the ukelele. It was broken beyond fixing.

Jerry started to jabber about how sorry he was, how he hadn't meant to do that, he just wanted to give us some good bass, et cetera, et cetera. I tried to shut him up and at the same time tried to get Lon to come on home.

After what seemed like a long time, I got Lon going up the road. Jerry stumbled around behind us, still yapping about how sorry he was and don't tell Dickie Poole. He kept trying to give us some of his damned fish. Finally I grabbed for the bucket and was about to throw his stupid fish in his face, when Lon grabbed my arm. "Let's get home," he said.

On the way up the path toward Grandmother's, I had one of my visions. I saw Mrs. Dodge, without a wheelchair or any injury, singing at Carnegie Hall. There were no words, but by her gestures you could see she was introducing someone. Out came Lon onto the stage, in white tie and tails. Tremendous applause from a full house. Then, with the most tragic gesture, he held up his broken ukelele in both hands.

Grandmother was still downstairs when we walked in. I realized that after the skirmish with Jerry, we smelled faintly of fish. She sniffed, and looked at the broken ukelele. "Have you boys been brawling again?" She said it in the driest, most casual tone, but I could feel the fury behind the manner. She was looking especially at Lon.

He returned the look. "My ukelele fell on a rock and got broken."

"Ah, well," she said, "I presume you can get another. It's not a Stradivarius, after all."

It must have been a full minute that Lon just looked at her without speaking. Neither one wavered. Then he said quietly, "No, hardly a Stradivarius. It was my mother's." He turned away and went upstairs.

For once I saw Grandmother at a loss. Finally she said, "Come in a minute, Charles."

I followed her into the living room. She paced for a few minutes, and finally said, "You seem to have come very much under the influence."

I was startled. For a second I thought she meant I was drunk. "What influence, Grandmother?"

"Your cousin."

"Oh. Well, I suppose we have influenced each other. Is that bad?"

Without answering the question she said, "While I was in New York I talked to the headmaster of Loomis School. He's the son of an old friend, and he thinks he might have a place for Lon."

I was stunned. I'd completely forgotten how I hoped she'd send him off to Country Day. But Lon to an American boarding school! Not that there aren't some good ones—and Loomis is a good one—but not for Lon. It would be cruel. "You mustn't do that, Grandmother."

Her eyebrows shot up, and her eyes got intensely blue. "Oh? And why not?"

"It would be awful for him." It was hard to explain. "I mean an American boarding school is so . . ."

"So American, perhaps?"

"Well, yes. An outsider would have a hard time. And especially Lon."

She looked really annoyed. "What is so special about Lon? He has had the Oriental part of his training; it is my duty to see that he gets the American part."

I was saying more than I'd ever said to her before.

"You don't apply culture like a club sandwich, Grandmother. He's having a hard enough time adjusting as it is . . ."

She flushed angrily. "And making it extraordinarily hard for everyone else. We've hardly had a normal day since he came."

I refrained from asking what a normal day was.

"He's upset your parents and the Hancocks, you, me, the whole town."

"It's not his fault if he's attacked by savages like the Parrish bunch. He was very brave and, in my opinion, very . . . Christian." I hesitated because it seemed like a strange word for me to use; I'm not given to describing people as Christian or not.

She sat on the sofa, her fingers fiddling very fast with the beading on the seat. "He has changed you, and I don't like it. Right now all your energies should be directed toward getting your West Point appointment . . ."

I took a deep breath. "I'm not going to West Point, Grandmother."

I wished I hadn't said it. She seemed to shrink a little and grow old as she sat there looking at me.

"Not going?"

"No. Even if they'd have me."

"May one ask why?"

"I want to help prevent wars, not join them. I'm going to be a writer."

The look she gave me was like getting struck by lightning. "Have you forgotten right and wrong? For centuries your ancestors on both sides have offered their strength and their lives to their country. They never presumed to put their own inclinations in first place, over the needs of their country. They knew what honor meant. No one likes war. War is a terrible scourge. But one cannot throw away honor and courage to save one's neck."

That made me mad. "I think it takes more courage to say no to war than to go along with the mob. You mention peace in this town and right away you're practically lynched. But what did Perry Haskell and Tom Terry ever find out about war? Or even Ray Hoffstetter, over there at Camp Edwards? There's Jerry Malone, of course, with his dishonorable discharge from the Navy—"

"I'm not talking about men like Malone."

"What do any of these guys know about war, what do any of them know, compared to what Lon has been through?"

"You are distorting the issue, Charles."

"The issue is very simple. One is either for war or against it." If my father could have heard me talking to my grandmother like that, he would have fainted. I almost fainted myself.

My grandmother leaned back. "I don't know you anymore."

I decided I'd better shut up.

She closed her eyes for a minute. Then they flew open, looking terribly angry and almost, it seemed to me, frightened. "I wish that boy had never set foot in this house!" she said.

133

And if Lon's door was open, there was a pretty good chance he heard her.

After I cooled off, I came back to say good night to Lon and make sure he was okay. That was the night he showed me his father's letter.

16

A FEW DAYS LATER WHEN I WAS ON MY WAY HOME FROM
the courts, Jerry Malone called me over to his shop. It was
past closing time and he'd been waiting for me. He was
sweeping the floor, which he'd already swept. As I came
up, he asked me how things were going, and that kind
of thing, all the time smiling as if I'm the face he's been
longing to see all day. A quick glance at the mirror told
me no miracle had occurred to my face. There was a
kind of bulky box sitting on the barber chair.

He rambled on, and I was getting impatient. Jerry
Malone obsequious was even worse than Jerry Malone
surly.

So I said, "Well, see you around," or one of those
brilliant bits of folk wisdom, and started to leave.

"Wait, Charles." He was very serious now. Jerry
Malone portentous. "Listen, Charles, I was really sorry
about what happened to the kid's uke. I mean it was an
accident pure and simple . . ."

" 'Simple' perhaps," I murmured, being my most nasty-superior, "but hardly 'pure.' "

He ignored my witticism, as people do. "Muldoon and I had a mite too much to drink . . ."

"A mite."

"You know how it is, a couple of guys fish all day and have a few . . ."

"I don't know. I'm under age."

"I'd hate to have a wrong impression get around . . ."

"You mean nobody loves a drunken barber."

He gave a very forced laugh. "Right. And you and I know I'm not that kind of a guy."

"Jerry," I said, and I wasn't being smart now; I was being truthful. "The kind of guy you are is a subject I'd just as soon not dwell on." I started out the door.

He was mad, but he rearranged his face very quickly. "Charles, I want you to take this package to Lon." He picked up the box in the chair.

"What is it?" I said. "A bomb?"

He took off the cover to show me. It was a ukelele. But any further similarity to Lon's instrument ended there. It was painted black, and it had a garish red and green picture of a Hawaiian girl, in a bikini, doing the hula.

"Good God," I said.

He took it that I was stunned with admiration. "Cute, isn't it? I got it over to Rochester. The kid'll love it."

"Sure," I said. "Look, Jerry, you'd better give it to him yourself." I walked back toward the sidewalk. For some reason not at all clear to me, the main thing Jerry seemed just then was pathetic.

When I saw Lon later, I told him about the ukelele.

He looked dismayed. "Well, all right. I'll stop by and thank him. I guess it was a nice gesture."

"It was a bribe."

He shrugged. "Let it go."

"Sometimes I think you're too forgiving; you're darn near meek!"

He smiled. "You know I'm not meek. Ask Joey Parrish."

A few nights later when we were coming home from a movie, I discovered he was terrified of firecrackers. It was getting close to the Fourth of July, and kids were already popping off firecrackers. Somebody threw a bunch right behind us, and Lon nearly jumped out of his skin. He grabbed my arm hard.

"Take it easy," I said. "It's only firecrackers."

He gave an embarrassed laugh and wiped his hand across his forehead. "Sorry. They always do that to me."

"How come?"

"It sounds too much like gunfire." He shook his head. "You'd think I'd be used to it by now."

"You'll probably never get used to it." I tried to imagine what it must have been like to have guns going off all around you for the first eight years of your life, knowing every time you took a step you might set off a land mine, and every time a plane went over you might get clobbered. It was impossible for me to imagine what his life must have been like, but every now and then, I got a hint.

We had two visitors at our house that night. One was Professor Harding, who was chairman that year of the

Lake Property Owners' Association. He was there to collect money for the fireworks. It was traditional on the night of the Fourth for the cottagers to set off fireworks all around the lake, and they planned it so the overall effect would be good. It was usually pretty spectacular, with rockets and stuff swooshing up over the lake.

The other visitor, after the professor, was Ray Hoffstetter. It was the fiftieth anniversary year of the Legion post, which had been named the William C. Miller Post for my great-grandfather, who was an infantry captain in World War I. The Legion guys wanted some kind of anniversary do, and they were trying to decide what. Ray was going to be in New York on business right up to the day before the Fourth, so in the end the Legion guys left it to Ray to dream up something while he was gone. He was at our house to check out various ideas with my father, because Ray's intention was to find some way to smooth out the irritation at the Millers that still floated around town. Ray was a peaceful guy and he liked us, and it distressed him.

"They need to remember what the Millers have done for this town," Ray kept saying.

I knew he meant well, but he made me uneasy. I thought the town needed a chance to forget about the Millers for a while. As far as I was concerned, they could change the name of the town to Parrish's Pothole.

But all such musings were forgotten by the next day, because *a* I received a letter from Patty saying they would be home in the fall and *b* I felt for the first time that my face looked a little better.

17

THE NIGHT BEFORE THE FOURTH WAS ALWAYS A BEEHIVE of activity. Everybody was getting ready for the parade, which was (wow!) even bigger and better than the Memorial Day parade, with a band imported from Nashua, some clowns from who knows where, and floats. There was a Legion float, a VFW float, the Daughters of Job float, the Eastern Star float, the St. Martin's Sodality float, the Boy Scouts float, et cetera. Everybody had crepe paper coming out of their hair, and glue all over themselves. Even the Flames were into the act, with red, white, and blue crepe paper covering their trail bikes.

My parents were working on the church float, carrying out the orders of the minister, who waved his hammer and was in his element. Boys shot off firecrackers all over, and little kids waved sparklers and got their balloons busted and howled. There were two balloon men, three ice-cream men, two hot dog men, and one cotton candy woman.

At eight o'clock that night there was the Legion affair at the Town Hall. I heard Ray had come in on the late plane at Logan and had just driven up. People were worrying about the floats because it looked like rain.

It was hot and steamy in the auditorium. By Ray's previous request the Millers sat en bloc in the second row. Grandmother was on the outside aisle, in case she felt unwell; then Mr. Hancock and Mrs. H., my mother, my father, Lon, and me. I was on the inside aisle, so I could spread out my legs, which never fit in a normal seat.

There was the singing of the "Star-Spangled Banner"; there was the prayer by Mr. Barnes; there was a speech by Perry Haskell paying tribute to "the dream of America"; there was a rendition of "America the Beautiful" by Miss Amy Robards from North Conway; there was a dance titled "Lexington and Concord" by the Campfire Girls, dressed in Revolutionary War costumes and audibly directed by Miss Verona Pritchett. It was getting hotter and hotter. I glanced at Lon and saw the sweat on his forehead. I leaned forward a little to check on Grandmother; she had her usual public appearance expression, pale, dignified, determined. But she had some new lines in her face. I thought we had better take her to Boston for a checkup at the Lahey Clinic.

The hall was full. Some humanitarian at the back opened the doors, and I saw Ray Hoffstetter tiptoe around the stage, opening the doors that led outside, while the children were dancing.

Finally Ray and Perry came back on stage, followed by the Legion Drum and Bugle Corps, who blasted us with "As the Caissons Go Rolling Along."

Then Ray stepped up to the mike. He had a flat package in his hands. He's a fairly painless speaker, because he keeps it short. He talked about the history of the post, and about Captain William C. Miller, who won this, that, and the other medal for distinguished service in the First World War. He mentioned the contributions made by other Miller's Lake men in various wars, and he spoke of Pete Bennett, our MIA in Vietnam.

He said, "In honor of all the men from Miller's Lake who have served in our country's wars and helped to make our country great and free, we of the William C. Miller Post wish to dedicate our new flag."

Pause while Ray fumbles with the package. I wished he'd get it over. There was some muttering going on at the back of the hall. All this talk about the Millers was just what they were sick of, and to tell the truth, I didn't blame them. There had been plenty of other people just as good, some better, in the history of Miller's Lake. Nobody ever mentioned my other grandfather, for instance; he wasn't allowed to go off to war because he was essential to the railroad. He worked like a dog all through the war, with too much responsibility, not enough help. They sang no sad songs for him.

Ray got the folded flag out of the box and he stood holding it like the minister holding the collection plate just before he blesses it. "Weather permitting, we will hold the flag-raising ceremony at eight tomorrow morning. But I would like to announce now, while you are all here, the name of the person whom we will ask to raise this dedicated flag." He paused.

I glanced at the family. Grandmother and Dad were frowning, so I knew they didn't know what he was going to say. Lon didn't seem to be listening, although he probably was. My mother threw me an anxious look.

"My attempt to get in touch with any of Peter Bennett's family failed, unfortunately. Therefore our plan to have two people raise the flag had to be altered. We now ask the son of one of our two recent war heroes if he will do the honors for us in the morning. Lon Miller." Ray beamed first at Grandmother and then at Lon.

Poor Ray. If he'd really worked at it, he couldn't have pulled a bigger boo-boo. Grandmother was leaning forward, clutching the arms of her chair. My father was, as the saying goes, slack-jawed. Lon sat as if he were in shock.

"Go up there, dear," my mother said to him.

He didn't move. There was a little smatter of applause, after the first stunned silence. Mr. Crane and his family clapped, and so did Doc Adams and Eloise Derby and her claque. Sarah from the Spa clapped and beamed. Some others joined in. We needed the Dodges badly, but they were in Bar Harbor for the Fourth. Dickie Poole kept the applause going a moment longer, but it was getting strained and Lon hadn't moved.

I began to get mad. I knew how he felt, and I admired his principles so much I was practically changing my whole life because of them, but there's a time to be pure and a time to meet people halfway. I gave him a hard nudge. "Get up there."

He gave me a startled look. I stood up so he had to go by me or else leave me standing there like a fool. He climbed past me and went up onto the stage, moving like somebody with tunnel vision. The applauders applauded again and Ray shook his hand enthusiastically, but there was some ominous muttering behind me.

Ray held out the flag, but Lon stepped away. He stood on the apron of the stage. He looked once at Grandmother, but after that he looked directly at me, a look that begged for understanding. I didn't respond to it. It didn't seem like the moment for empathy.

Lon began to speak in a low voice. "I appreciate your thoughtfulness in wanting to honor my father . . ." Someone in the back yelled "louder" but Lon didn't seem to hear him. "I really do. But you are remembering him as a man of war. I remember him—and he wished to be remembered—as a man of peace." He looked at Ray, as if just realizing he was there. "Thank you . . . I'm sorry."

Ray tried to say something to him, but Lon shook his head and bolted out the stage door. I was suddenly ashamed of being unsympathetic. I'd let him down. There was a big and growing commotion in the hall then, some laughter, some jeering, a little applause.

Grandmother got to her feet, and I was scared she was going to say something. Grandmother, like Lon, didn't know how to meet people halfway. I untangled my legs and got myself up on the stage before I had any idea of what I was going to do. I saw Grandmother going out the side door with Mr. and Mrs. Hancock. I held up my arms to the crowd.

If there's one thing I am, it's visible. Standing up on a stage with my arms lifted straight up, I must have looked twenty-five feet tall. There were some yells and taunts, but I just stood there until they got quiet out of curiosity. I was nervous but I remembered my debating club technique.

When they were quiet, I said, "I hope I'm not presumptuous if I thank the Legion in behalf of my family for their gesture." They were listening, I suppose about half of them hoping and expecting I'd say something stupid. "I'm sure you understand my cousin Lon's reaction . . ." Somebody booed. I ignored it. "War is terribly real to him, in a way that most of us have no idea of." There was still some racket at the back of the room. Somebody shushed them. Dickie Poole walked up the aisle and stood at the back. The noise died down. "For the first eight years of his life he lived with the sound not of firecrackers but of gunfire. Our kids aim sticks at each other and say, 'You're dead.' All around him were people who were really shot dead. Our kids say *'Over the river and through the woods, to Grandmother's house we go.'* He went to his grandparents' house just in time to see it blown up. He saw his mother wounded, later dying of her wound. His father was killed when a village he was working to rebuild was accidentally bombed by our aircraft." I paused for a second. They were listening. I hoped I wouldn't get too carried away. You can get hooked on a listening audience. But I really desperately wanted them to understand, at least some of them.

"Lon said just now that his father wanted to be remembered as a man of peace. Bill Miller stayed in Vietnam longer than he had to, because he'd gotten a chance to help rebuild. He left a letter for his son, and I hope Lon will forgive me if I tell you one thing that letter said. 'We have been a family of warriors,' he said, 'each of them a brave man doing what seemed to him the honorable thing. But I believe with all my heart that all war is wicked. The time has come to stop it.' " I was quoting Uncle Bill's letter from memory. And because I thought people were really hearing me now, I decided to add one thing more, "He ended by saying, 'On your mother's side there's at least one poet I know of, and a French philosopher. Cleave to the poets and the philosophers, Lon. There must be an end to killing.' "

I stopped, praying I hadn't betrayed Lon's confidence too far. The audience was very quiet. Then some people left. I felt terrible. For a minute I'd really hoped I'd reached them. I started to leave the stage. My parents were both crying quietly.

Before I got off, Dickie Poole came down the aisle and jumped up on the stage. "I'd like to propose," he said, "that the Legion dedicate this new flag to peace. Our flag was never meant to stand for war. Let's make a start at peace."

Ray shook his hand, and there was quite a burst of applause. I saw Jerry Malone, not clapping, not leaving, trying to play it safe. Others were just sitting there,

145

and I couldn't tell what they thought. Then Mr. Crane got to his feet.

"I am in favor of Dickie's suggestion," he said. He remained standing, and his wife and kids stood up too.

"Add my vote," said Doc Adams, standing up like some wonderful old scarecrow.

Sarah stood up, all four feet ten of her. "Can a lady vote?"

Laughter and applause. Then a whole bunch of people were getting on their feet. Eloise and her chums. Harry North and his whole family. Johnny Pritchett and a couple of other kids he was with. Harold Bumpus' mother stood up, and hauled Harold up practically by the collar. Ralph Deschamps stood up. Orval Jones and his family stood up. Way at the back of the hall, where she could make a quick getaway if necessary, Myrtle Lightbody stood up and waved.

Mrs. Muldoon and Mr. Muldoon and all the little Muldoons made a noisy exit. The George Thaxters stayed. About half the Flames left, the others stayed, maybe hoping for a fight somewhere, somehow.

I'd say about fifty percent of the original crowd was standing. I felt very goose-bumpy. Then, I guess at a word from Ray, the Drum and Bugle Corps filed back onto the stage and played "America the Beautiful." I'd have given anything if Lon and Grandmother had been there. The crowd joined in, singing the words of the song. When it was over, Ray shook my hand very hard and said something I didn't hear. Dickie shook my hand and said, "Your Uncle Bill would have been proud of you both."

When we got home, I went over to Grandmother's right away. I had to make them both understand what had happened.

The Hancocks were in the kitchen looking depressed. "She's in her room," Mrs. H. said. "Resting, Charles."

"I won't bother her but a minute. Things turned out pretty good, at the meeting."

"That's good, dear."

I could tell they weren't at all reassured. I went upstairs to Grandmother's room and knocked. There was such a long pause before she said "Come in," I thought she must be asleep. She was in her housecoat, standing by the bureau where Grandfather's and Uncle Bill's pictures were.

Grandmother turned away from me and sat in the wing chair by the casement windows, looking out across the meadow. She looked awfully white and tired. Now that I was here, I didn't know what to say. I'd been so carried away with my own oratory, I'd forgotten that she probably wouldn't have liked it.

"Things turned out better than it looked as if they were going to," I said, feebly.

"That's good." She sounded far off. There was a long silence. I wondered if I should just leave. Then she said, "It's gone past me now. Gone past like a river."

I wasn't sure what she meant, but it sounded poetic. She gave a little jump, and her hand grabbed the arm of the chair. Her hand looked awfully white and trembly.

She caught her breath.

"Are you all right, Grandmother?"

After a minute she said, "Dear, give me the little bottle on my bedside table."

I got it. She took a tiny white pill from it and gave me back the bottle. It was Dr. Adams' prescription for nitroglycerin tablets. "Use sublingually in case of pain, for angina." I never knew she had angina.

She had her eyes closed, and her face was tense. She was breathing in a gaspy kind of way.

"Shall I help you into bed?"

She shook her head. Then she winced with pain. "Call him . . ." she said.

18

I BUMPED INTO LON IN THE HALL, LITERALLY. HE'D JUST come down the hall from his room. I was so scared about Grandmother I was hardly aware of him.

"Charles," he said, "I've got to talk to you . . ."

I shoved him out of the way and flew down the stairs to the kitchen, to call Doc Adams and alert the Hancocks. Very vaguely in the back of my mind I heard the front door shut, but I didn't give it a thought.

The Hancocks, who knew about the angina (the only ones who did, it turned out), went into action. Mrs. H. raced upstairs, and Mr. H. got a bottle of brandy from the pantry. I got Doc Adams right away, and he said, "I'm on my way, Charles."

I ran over and told my parents, and the three of us spent the next hour or so pacing around the house, getting in each other's way, cross-examining Doc Adams whenever he came out of Grandmother's room. My father kept talking about the hospital, intensive care. My mother kept a big kettle of water boiling on the stove.

Doc Adams finally came into the kitchen and said she felt better. "I'm not going to haul her way to Rochester, in Fourth of July traffic, to the hospital. It's not a blockage, I'm sure of that. It's just an unusually severe attack of angina. I *told* her not to go to the Town Hall. With angina you shouldn't go around getting too mad or glad or sad. It raises holy ned with the arteries." He put his arm around my mother. "Mildred, what are you going to do with all that hot water? She's not having a baby." He laughed and hugged her. "I'll tell you what: you can use it to make us a pot of your good coffee. All right?"

While they were sitting around drinking the coffee, Mrs. Hancock called me out into the hall. She looked frightened.

"Is Grandmother worse?"

"No. She's asleep. But Charles, Lon is gone."

"What do you mean, gone?"

"He's gone." She began to cry.

"Oh, he'll be back. I doubt if he even knew Grandmother was sick. I heard the front door close just before I called the doctor. Don't worry about Lon."

"He's gone," she said. "His mother's picture is gone."

I just stared at her for a minute. It was almost eleven; I was too groggy from everything that had happened to be very quick on the trigger. Then I ran upstairs.

She was right. Lon's mother's picture was gone, and his jacket. His other clothes were there, and his books and things. But the picture—that worried me. I found Mrs. H. waiting for me in the hall.

"Don't panic. He didn't take his clothes and stuff."

"I'm worried. He was so upset."

"Look, I'll find him. He couldn't go anywhere at this hour. Cover for me. Don't let the others know. We'll be back soon." I went out the front door, got the car keys at our house, and set out to find my cousin.

The only way to get out of town without a car was to go out to the highway and hitch a ride. I drove slowly out the gravel road that connected with the highway a couple of miles from town. Anybody could have ducked into the trees and I wouldn't have seen them on that dark country road, but there was no one in sight. I cruised south on the highway for a couple of miles, and then back a few miles toward the north. Nothing but a few cars zipping along.

I bumped over the deserted stretch of road that connected with the old highway. It was almost unnavigable, with all the hardtop that had buckled and cracked. I hoped I wouldn't break a spring.

I drove slowly along the old highway, past some parked cars with kids making out (if they recognized the car, I could imagine them saying, "God! can't you get away from the Millers *anywhere*?"), past the Flames' clubhouse, which Dickie Poole had padlocked, and down the main street of the town. Quite a few people were still hanging around, shooting off rockets and whatnot. Sarah's Spa was filled, and the bars were busy. I saw Mr. Lightbody staggering along by himself, waving his arms and talking a blue streak.

I knew Lon wouldn't be where the action was. I drove to the lake and unlocked the boathouse with my father's key; Lon had mine. He had apparently used it, because the canoe was gone. I got out the outboard and started down the lake.

I was trying very hard to think myself into Lon's mind. He undoubtedly felt we all disapproved of his refusal of the flag; he'd mind it the worst from me because I usually agreed with him.

Lon probably had had no idea that Grandmother was ill, and when I shoved him out of the way in the hall, he probably took it that I was still angry and rejected him. I wished I'd taken a second to explain, but I'd been too scared. So Lon must have decided to clear out. Temporarily or permanently? That question worried me. You don't take your mother's picture if you're just going to paddle around the lake.

He knew the Dodges were in Maine, so he wouldn't be going there. I doubted if he would anyway; he was too proud to ask for help even from his friends. I felt he must be at the cottage.

It was a very dark, cloudy night, and when I came by the big island, suddenly the whole lakeshore lit up in a great blaze of shooting light. At the same time I heard the town clock striking midnight. The cottagers, on signal, were shooting off their fireworks. It was really eerie to be out there in the middle of that black water with all those brilliant rockets and shooting stars and stuff going up into the sky all around me. I could hear the hiss as some of the fireworks nearest me sailed up into the sky, and then the little pop as they burst into brilliant colors and designs, and then again the soft sigh as they went out almost at once and fell back toward the lake.

I would have enjoyed it if I hadn't been worried about Lon. As I came toward our cottage, I saw the fireworks going up at the Dodge place, but I knew they had asked one of the Terry boys to set them off, so as not to spoil the effect.

Mr. Hancock and my father had been down at our cottage in the morning to set up our fireworks, but now of course they had Grandmother on their minds. I kept hoping I'd see our rockets go off, though, because it would mean Lon was there. But that little stretch of shore stayed dark.

I cut the engine and drifted into the place where we tied up the boat, jumped up on the cement wall, and tied her up. If Lon wasn't there, I didn't know where to look.

As I came along the path, the cottage was almost invisible in the dark setting of trees, and behind it the woods looked very black. "The woods are lovely, dark and deep"—was that the way that line went?

I stood on the steps and looked at the silent cottage. Behind me the wash from my boat was still slapping up on the shore. I called him. My voice seemed to get swallowed up right away in the dense darkness. Behind me the fireworks still shot up into the sky, one moment brilliant and vivid, the next moment gone. I thought of the times when I was a little kid, out on the dock watching the fireworks and thrilled out of my mind. I envied that little kid. At what age, I wondered, did you stop living just in the moment? When did all the worry start?

The cottage door was seldom locked. I went inside, wondering if Lon could be hiding. I flicked my flashlight around the room. That model boat of Uncle Bill's was on the table, and it had not been there before. He'd been at the cottage then. I called and called, and I went upstairs and down. There was no other sign.

I began to feel exasperated. Why this wild-goose chase? I should go home and let him come when he felt like it. I wasn't his mother.

I picked up the boat. A piece of the rigging that had come loose had been newly tied; you could tell because the place where the old knot had been was lighter than the rest. Why did he care so much about that old boat? Then it came to me where he was. I don't know why, but I knew. I put the boat down and ran out of the cottage. I passed the rockets that were braced between rocks, pointing skyward. On a crazy impulse I struck a match and lit the fuses of three of them. The Miller place wouldn't be entirely dark.

The first one went off as I cast off in the boat and spun the starter. It didn't go very high. There was a brief falling shower of red and blue stars and then it fizzled out. The second one lifted off the ground about six feet and fell into the lake with a hiss. I kept looking back for the third one. Just when I'd given it up, it went off. It was a beauty. It went up and up and up, and then burst in a great shower of red and purple and green and blue stars, and just as they faded, new bursts came from the rocket. It was really splendid. I felt better.

I opened the boat up full throttle and took her down around the point to the end of the lake, where I beached the boat. The canoe was there, and I started down the dirt road toward the mill, running. I crossed the tracks and took the low path around the hill to the millpond. It was so dark in there I couldn't see a thing at first. I could barely make out the big circle of the mill wheel and then the shadowy, ghostly outline of the burned-out mill. For some reason I thought of that cathedral at Coventry, where Lon's mother had gone.

I called Lon, but there was no answer. My voice sounded smothered in that enclosed place. I went around the pond to the mill and looked up. Lon was at the very top of the skeleton stairway, above the trees, with the black surface of the pond below him. I remembered his saying, "From the top you could dive right into the millpond." And I'd said, "If you wanted to break your neck."

"Lon." I was surprised that my voice sounded so calm. "Half in love with easeful Death . . .," he'd quoted that first day. "Come on down, Lon. That's not safe." Not safe. I wondered if he'd laugh.

"Go away, Charles." His voice sounded hoarse, as if he'd been crying.

"No, not without you. It's late, Lon. Come on home."
"No."

I waited a minute, but he didn't move. I said, "I'm coming up." I started up that lousy stairway. I'd never thought I'd ever climb that thing to the top, but I couldn't think of any other way to get Lon down. I was terrified that he was going to dive off into the pond.

I was all the way up to the first landing when he said, "Go down. I'm coming down."

I nearly fell down the stairs in relief. My muscles were trembling, as if I'd run a couple of miles. What a neurotic.

He came down quickly and easily, as if it were nothing. He looked at me a moment, and then he sat down on a fallen timber. "Go home. I'll be all right." He sat kind of huddled up, and I sat down beside him. We stayed there for quite a while in silence. It was getting definitely chilly. I shivered and moved a little and felt something large and hard in his jacket pocket. I couldn't think for a second what it might be, but then I thought of his mother's picture. I wondered if he had really meant to jump. I looked at the dark, still water of the pond and shivered again, but not from cold. It was probably not more than three feet deep even in the middle.

"Well," I said, "shall we shove off? It's late; time to go home."

"I haven't got any home." He hadn't looked at me since he sat down.

"Of course you have. Your home is with us, at my house. That's where you belong." I hadn't even thought of it till I said it, but of course it was true; it was where he should have been all along. I knew my parents would agree. If Grandmother objected, I would have to handle that; but the way things were, she'd probably be relieved.

Lon had turned to look at me. "How can that be?"

"Because I say so." I laughed, to take the edge off the arrogance, but I meant it. It was time I began to take some responsibility for the Millers.

156

"Grandmother wouldn't stand for it," he said. And he added, a little bitterly, "I'd distract you from your pursuit of West Point."

"I'm not going to West Point. I've withdrawn my application."

He straightened. "Annapolis?"

"No. I'm going to travel and write."

He looked at me a long time. "Does Grandmother know?"

"I told her."

"Wow," he said softly. "Wow."

I stood up. "We'd better get back. Grandmother had an angina attack."

He sounded startled. "What's that?"

"Heart."

He gave a little groan and buried his face in his hands. "I did it. I upset her."

"Lon, get up." I sounded sharper than I meant to. He stood up. "Stop seeing yourself as the cause of everything. There are more things going on in Grandmother's mind than just you."

"I know that." He sounded wounded, but I was glad I'd said it. At fourteen or fifteen you do get to feeling that all the world revolves around you. I knew; I'd just been there.

"Anyway, she's apparently had angina quite a while."

"We'd better go." He led the way around the pond and down the path to the boat landing. We hitched the canoe to the outboard and went home. As we came around the curve of the shore, Billy Terry set off the last rocket at the Dodge place. They always had the last one, the traditional set piece of the American flag. We watched it light up the dark sky and seem to flutter, like a real flag in a slight breeze. It looked very pretty and not at all militant. Lon sat with his head back looking up at it till it winked out, leaving that second when you still see the outline without the color, or maybe it's just the impression left on the retina.

"That was pretty," I said.

"I don't trust flags," Lon said.

The lights in the cottages twinkled like stars, far away from us. On the lake there was no light except the narrow beam of our boat light. "Well, a flag is just a symbol," I said. "It's not an absolute unchanging truth or anything. A symbol is only what people make it."

He didn't say anything until we docked at the boathouse. "Is Grandmother going to be okay?"

"Dr. Adams says she is. But I guess you never know with hearts."

When we drove into our yard, I told Lon he could go in; I'd just run across the field and let Mrs. Hancock know we were home, and check on Grandmother.

"I'll go with you."

My father came out as we stopped. I could see my mother in the doorway. I had a sudden moment of panic. "Is Grandmother all right?"

"Yes, she's asleep," my father said. He looked awfully tired.

Before I got the garage doors shut, Mr. Hancock came running across the meadow, his long body looking like Ichabod Crane in the dark. "Is Lon with you?" he said.

Then he saw Lon and his face relaxed. "Oh, fine. I'll go tell the Mrs." He gave Lon an awkward pat and took off again.

"Lon is going to move in with us," I said to my father.

"Of course," he said. "We'll get his things in the morning. You boys better get to bed. It's late."

My mother smiled at Lon as we came into the kitchen. "I hope you're a sound sleeper. Charles thrashes around so. Tomorrow we'll turn the front bedroom into your room."

Lon gave her a smile and he started to speak, but he choked up. My mother hugged him, and he hugged her, hard.

I stood on the lower step of the staircase and lifted my arm. "Come, thou black knight, or I shall smite thee so dolorous a stroke as shall cleave thy shield and thy helmet and even to the bone of thy brain pan."

Lon laughed.

19

IT WAS MY MOTHER WHO TOLD GRANDMOTHER THAT LON was moving in with us. She never said anything about the conversation, but she came back humming something in her wild off-key way.

At dinner that night she told us that Grandmother wanted to go to London as soon as Dr. Adams approved. She had a favorite cousin in London whom she visited from time to time.

"She thinks she might stay the winter," my mother said, "if the weather isn't too awful. If it is, she might go to Florence."

"Oh, she'll have a good time," my father said. "She can go to the opera. Lon, have some more chicken."

Lon and my mother had already fixed up the big front bedroom with the bay windows that looked out over the meadow. It already looked so much like Lon's place, it was hard to remember when it was a guest room.

Lon still worked for Mr. Hancock every morning, and in the afternoons he worked for Mrs. Dodge in her garden. She liked to stay down at the cottage a lot, so she needed somebody at the house in town. Lon seemed happier or more contented than I had ever seen him.

I didn't see Grandmother for more than a few minutes at a time until just before she left for London. At first she had had to rest a lot, and then she'd spent a week in Boston at the hospital having a whole lot of tests.

A couple of nights before she was to go, she summoned both Lon and me. I wasn't sure Lon had seen her at all since the Fourth, but you never knew such things unless Lon chose to speak of them, and he usually didn't.

Grandmother was sitting in the wing chair in her bedroom. Her big suitcase was open on the luggage stand. She looked a lot better, and kind of pleased and excited. I suppose it seemed good to be getting away from all of us for a while.

Lon was stiff and silent after the obligatory "Good evening, Grandmother" bit. I began to feel nervous myself, though I don't know why. She looked at us both for a minute, which did nothing to relax us, even though she did not look hostile at all.

"Are you contented in your new home?" she said to Lon.

"Yes, thank you."

"Charles doesn't bully you?" She gave me a quick little smile, to indicate it was a joke.

Lon smiled, but not too successfully. "He's very good."

She looked at me with those fantastic blue eyes. "Yes, Charles is good. He is quick-tempered, like all the Millers, but he is not stubborn nor excessively proud. As you are."

I caught my breath. Was she going to lambaste poor Lon after all? I couldn't look at him, but I felt him stiffen.

"As your father was," Grandmother said. She paused. "And as I am."

I felt the tension ease out of Lon; I heard him let out his breath.

"I think the word is 'hubris,'" Grandmother said. "Ask Charles; he's the classics scholar." She paused. "Your father and I did constant battle, you know. And you and I would do the same, I'm afraid. Yes, you are overproud, like my side of the family."

Lon finally spoke. "My mother also had great pride."

Grandmother gave a little start, as if maybe in making the gesture of accepting him as a Miller, or a Thorndike-Miller, she had unconsciously tried to shut out the rest of his background, and now he was pointing it out to her. I felt sorry for her; she'd made such a good try. But of course he couldn't let it go that he was all Miller.

Grandmother put her hand to her face, and for a minute she didn't speak. Then she said, "Yes, I suppose she was. Bill would have chosen someone with spirit." She looked up at him. "Is Mr. Hancock downstairs?"

"Yes."

"Ask him, please, if he will go up in the attic and find your father's old mandolin. I would like you to have it."

I looked at Lon now. His face was really lit up, luminous. But all he said was, "Thank you very much." He almost bounded out of the room.

"Well, Charles," Grandmother said, "are you going to be a very good writer? We don't tolerate mediocrities, you know." She was smiling a little.

"Very good indeed. Of course the world may not recognize it right away. I may die unheralded and unsung, like Melville, but I'll be happy."

She snorted. "Nonsense. Melville was miserable. You'd better see to it that you're heralded and sung. Your great-grandfather knew Melville, you know."

"No, I did not know. No one ever tells me anything."

"Until lately you haven't been old enough to need telling." She put out her hand. "Take care of everyone while I'm gone."

All at once I really hated to have her go away. What if something happened to her? "One of us ought to go with you," I said.

"Don't be absurd. I'm good for years yet."

"I didn't mean that . . ."

"Yes, you did, and I appreciate your concern. But Charles, I am an independent woman."

I had to laugh. "I know that, Grandmother." I leaned down and kissed her. "Please have a wonderful time."

"Of course. And Charles, don't let your thinking get sloppy. And do see what you can do about Lon."

I didn't ask her what I was supposed to do about him. It was time to go, but I still hung around, hating to leave her.

"I do believe, Charles, that you are filling out."

"About time."

"Ah, time is what you have."

At that moment, from downstairs in the kitchen, we could hear the faint plink of a mandolin. Grandmother listened, and her face got terribly sad.

"Grandmother," I said, "I know you hate mushy statements, but I would like to say that I am very, very fond of you."

She gave me a long, steady look. "Thank you, Charles." Her voice was very cool, but her mouth trembled a little. "I shall treasure that particular mushy statement. I am fond of you, too, as you know." She got up with her old energy. "And now I must finish packing."

I left her then. Four months later she died in London, of a heart attack. In her will she left her house and everything in it to me, except for anything that had been Uncle Bill's, which went to Lon. The money was left equally to my father, Lon, and me.

When I graduate from high school next month, I will take off for a year of travel. I was going to say haphazard, but it isn't haphazard at all; I've been planning it for years. The Hancocks will keep my house open for me. When Lon graduates, he plans to get a degree in agriculture and then return to his own country to help restore it. My father has a new project; he has plans for a small vocational school, where kids can learn carpentry, plumbing, and things like that. No tuition, but the kids will be asked to contribute something when they graduate and get a job. He's talked to different guys who have agreed to teach free—Jackson the plumber, and

Billy Halliday the welder and blacksmith, Peter and Ernie Bridges the carpenters, Jerry Malone the barber, and so on. Muldoon wants to teach a class in fly-tying. Maybe he'll stay sober enough to do it. Mrs. Bumpus wants Harold to enroll; he's dropped out of high school. Harold says he might be a welder. Dickie Poole has offered to turn everybody into milkmen, and Mr. Dodge will teach a course in banking if anyone wants it. My mother will teach cooking and sewing.

I hope Grandmother would approve of the ends to which her money has been put. She might not exactly approve, but she would have to admit we're all doing what we think is right.

The Parrishes moved to Ossipee Center. Nobody cried.

And so it goes, and so it goes. I'll send you a postcard from Rome.